Bill the Fly

1.

It was a bright, sunny morning in June when Bill first visited Jacob Kingsley. He flew in through the open window, buzzed about the room awhile, and then planted his six tiny legs along the wall opposite the bed.

Jacob opened his eyes with a yawn and stretched his large arms. He was a bachelor in his thirties, and looked the part. His face was unshaven, and he allowed his hair to grow and twist in whichever way it wanted. He hadn't had decent hygiene for a long time, not since Maddy. She had left him five months before, citing his "lack of motivation" as the catalyst. Maybe there was something to that, but Jacob thought that her moving in with her boss at the advertising agency directly after dumping him put her reasons for leaving into question.

The clock on the nightstand shone a bright red 10:00. He was three hours late already. Motivated by a lack of funds, he had taken a job at a textile factory nearby. He'd aced the walk-in interview. The manager thought him overqualified, but Jacob assured him that he was good for the job. He didn't have the patience or time to find anything else. The rent for his one-bedroom apartment was oddly expensive, especially for a town as small as Brandon. Jacob figured he wasn't far enough away from Phoenix for the prices to start dropping, even though there was nothing but dry, lonely desert for miles around.

The work at the factory was mind-numbing, but he rather liked it. There was something beautiful in the steady clanking of the machines. Once you got a rhythm going, the time went by quickly. He found it went by even quicker when he stared at the fine form of Emily Grainger. She was a petite brunette with hair always back in a ponytail. Green eyes hid behind her plastic safety goggles, with just a hint of pink lipstick on her pursed lips. The best part about her was that she looked nothing like Maddy. Word was that she had fled from a homicidally-inclined ex-husband who lived back east. Maybe Delaware? Jacob wasn't sure.

As he climbed out of bed and his feet touched the shag carpet floor, he scratched his fledgling beard and noticed the piercing chime. He brought his hand down on top of the large button on the alarm clock, silencing it and narrowly missing a small fly that clung to the button's edge.

"Shit," he said, and walked to the open window.

He poked his head outside and took a deep breath. The Arizona air wasn't like the air back east. It was dryer, and it clung to your nostrils and throat.

It would have been tolerable if it didn't also carry the subtle stench of what Jacob believed to be animal excrement.

"Coyote shit," he muttered under his breath, and slammed the window shut.

The fly buzzed by his ear as he walked to the bathroom, and he tried to smash it between his two enormous hands. He missed, and grunted his disapproval. He turned the faucet over the sink and cringed as it squeaked open.

"You'll have to try harder than that next time," a voice said. It was a deep, throaty voice.

Jacob spun around quickly, but saw no one. He shook his head and laughed a little before turning back to the sink and splashing water on his face. When he had finished, he walked to the toilet to relieve himself. The fly flew just above his head, taking off from its perch on the mirror in front of him. Wildly, Jacob threw his arms above him in a vain attempt to clip it. A loud chuckle echoed off the linoleum tile.

"Who's there?" Jacob shouted. He had heard about criminals bugging people's houses—hacking into computers, spying through webcams, and waiting until their unsuspecting victims took off their clothes. This had to be one of those.

"No one wants to see that, Jacob. There's no need to worry," the voice said.

The fly landed on the tip of Jacob's left elbow and crawled steadily up his arm.

"You would be amusing if you weren't so sad," the fly said.

Jacob lurched backward, producing a few guttural cries and banging his tailbone against the bathroom counter's edge. Several thoughts went through his mind. The first and most obvious one was that he was crazy. Bat-shit, off-your-rocker, talking-to-insects crazy. The second was that there must be some intruder hiding somewhere in the room playing tricks on him. Maybe he was hiding in his closet or under his bed, snickering. That was his second thought, but he dismissed it, realizing that it was the thought of a crazy person, so really it was linked to thought number one. The third was that those damn webcam-hacking perverts had got to him through some tiny, fly-shaped hacking device.

"I'm real. Let's clear that up right away," the fly said. "The sooner you accept that, the sooner we can move on."

"H-how?" Jacob stammered, surprised that he was actually going into discourse with a fly.

The fly twitched and answered. "I was born in a rotten grammar book. In my pupae stage I ate through nearly a dozen pages. Luckily, I got a good mix of the vocabulary, phonetic, and grammar sections so I came out able to grasp the English language rather well. Most of my siblings did not. My sister, unfortunately, knows only the vowels, though she does forget the y's sometimes."

Jacob stared at the fly on his arm, and it cocked its head and rubbed its red compound eye with its tiny front leg.

"Or I am not really a fly," it continued, "but a creature from another planet, dimension, plane, what-have-you, and I require your assistance to ward off an ancient evil eons in the making. Or I am one of your incessant web-cam perverts, just like you thought."

It crawled up to Jacob's shoulder and said much slower, "You can call me Bill."

2.

Jacob's morning routine was always dreadfully inadequate, but it was even more so that morning due to the frazzled state of what he believed to be his deteriorating brain. He stormed out of the bathroom, dressed only in his boxers, and immediately went to the closet for his black work boots. When the laces were sufficiently tight upon his foot, he reached up to his knee to fold his trousers down over them. It was then that he realized his crucial error. He got down on his hands and knees and looked under the bed for his regulation trousers, since he knew he had lazily discarded them some time after his fifth beer the night before. Bill flew off his arm and landed on top of Jacob's sweat-stained duvet.

"You took them off in the living room," he said. "Don't you remember?"

Jacob had forgotten. He got up off his knees and stamped into the living room, ignoring Bill, who lifted his tiny body off the bed and buzzed about Jacob's ear. *Maybe, if I ignore it, the thing will go away,* Jacob thought, and he reaffirmed himself in his actions.

Jacob stopped when he arrived at the archway to the living room, and surveyed the potato chip crumbs, empty beer cans, and crusty magazines that framed his large 1080p TV like a medieval king gazing upon his hunting grounds. He smiled. His desolate living room was the place he felt most free to be himself. Beneath the sunken faux suede couch protruded a dark bit of cloth, and, with a grunt, he bent down and took it in his fist. He tugged, but it would not give.

"They appear to be stuck," Bill said, landing on the crest of a particularly large sag in the couch.

"I know that," Jacob almost answered, but he caught himself, muttering only a garbled, "Ah Nugh."

"What was that?" Bill asked.

Jacob grasped the pants' leg with his other hand and pulled much harder this time. The couch creaked violently, and he worried that it might break. It had taken him nearly an entire afternoon and more than an ounce of brain power to get the monster inside the apartment, and he certainly didn't want all of that exertion to go to waste. Switching tactics, he began maneuvering the leg horizontally against the thick beige carpet, wiggling it back and forth until the couch began to relinquish its iron grip.

"Close now," Bill said.

Jacob eyed the fly cautiously as the trousers flew out from under the couch and into Jacob's expectant arms. He stood clumsily to his feet and put them on, slightly dismayed when he noticed a small tear near the right cuff. He wished he had a needle and thread, and that he knew how to use either of them. Then the pants could be mended, and he would still get in before lunch. He'd be a few yards behind on his work, but it wouldn't be anything Mr. Jay could be angry about.

Having already mentally put himself at arriving around noon, Jacob decided that he was hungry, and there was no use going to work on an empty stomach when it could be helped.

"Scrambled, right?" Bill said from the kitchen.

A frying pan filled with scrambled eggs was bubbling on the stove of the kitchenette. As Jacob walked onto the linoleum floor, two browned pieces of toast popped up from the toaster on the counter next to the percolating coffee pot. The aroma of crisping bacon flooded his nostrils, and he noticed that a smaller frying pan on the other burner was nearly finished cooking four long strips.

"How did you?" Jacob asked before his voice trailed off, standing dumbfounded between the center island and the kitchenette.

"I know you like apple butter with your toast," Bill said cheerily as he perched alongside the tan line of cabinetry. "It's already on the table."

Jacob glanced past the center island to the small card table he had made his dining place. It sat scrunched against the wall by the front door, one entire side completely unusable. A single lawn chair was unfolded against it, ensuring that its user would have a clear view of the television in the living room. At this place sat an open jar of apple butter and a full glass of orange juice—no pulp, just the way Jacob liked it.

He got himself a plate from the cabinet and filled it with the bacon, eggs, and toast as Bill buzzed happily about the kitchen. After pouring himself a large mug of coffee from the carafe, drowning it in cream and heaps of sugar, Jacob walked to the table and sat down in the lounge chair, maneuvering his body into a somewhat comfortable position before taking up his knife and fork in gleeful ecstasy.

"Everything to your liking?" Bill asked, resting on the tip of the orange juice glass.

"Yes, very," Jacob replied with a mouth full of some combination of toast, bacon, eggs, and coffee. He briefly swatted at Bill to get him to relinquish his post, and then drained half the glass of orange juice in one monstrous gulp.

"Well, I'm glad we're on speaking terms at last," Bill said as he landed in the middle of the table.

"I don't know about that," Jacob replied.

"I do. Now, after breakfast why don't we swing by that store on Katelyn and pick up some flowers for Emily? I'm sure she would appreciate it. Her feminine sensibilities are probably atrophying in that dusty old factory."

"Who's Emily?" Jacob gulped.

"Don't play coy with me. You have her name plastered all over your employee handbook in your locker. Some might call you too old for such games, but I don't judge. I give you the courtesy to be yourself and I don't ask questions. I hope that you can give me the same courtesy."

Jacob thought back to the handbook, and hoped that Bill wasn't aware of the particularly egregious pencil-sketch he had made of Emily in the nude that adorned the right margin of page 287. Of course Jacob had never seen her in such a way, but, judging from the generous way her work shirt bulged at the chest, he thought he got it about right.

"She's never even spoken to me," Jacob admitted, and the admission hurt a little.

"And how can we ratify that?"

"Not by giving her flowers like some kind of creep."

"It's not about the flowers. The flowers aren't the point. The point is the effort, Jacob. The point is that we are making an effort to be in her life. We are exerting ourselves to care about her. If we come on a little too strong, that's alright. She'll just think we care too strongly, which, I'm sure you'll agree, is not a problem at all. You cannot lose from trying."

Some of what the fly was saying made sense. "Why do you care? You're a fly," Jacob said, angrily rising from his chair at the notion that, perhaps, his romantic failure with Emily was due to his lack of motivation. He thought of Maddy and that made him angrier.

"Because," Bill said, "I have exerted myself to be in your life. I care about you. I want only what's best—for the both of us."

"What's best for both of us?"

Bill flew off and made his way through the hallway into the bedroom. "Come," he shouted. "Brush your teeth. You'll be late, and Emily is waiting."

3.

Bill was nowhere to be seen by the time Jacob slid into the cab of his blue pickup truck, but, as he turned the key, he thought he heard a faint buzzing sound. The engine churned to life, but he killed it in order to listen. The crackling under the hood slowly died into silence. No buzz. He started the truck back up and backed out of the driveway, shaking his head casually from side to side as a slight, nervous grin cut through his face.

So the magical talking fly was gone—disappeared sometime between brushing his teeth and that shot of bourbon before walking out the door. *Good. Good riddance,* he thought. Now maybe he could focus on work without giving into delusions. Bill *was* a delusion—probably brought on by overwork. As Jacob turned onto Grissom Street, he mentally noted that he'd have to put in a paid time-off request. Mr. Jay was working him to the bone, affecting his brain.

The tiny mom and pop gas station loomed directly ahead on the right. Its tired plywood sign was propped up on the roof by steel elbows and read, "Javelina Good Time." It was a terrible pun, and it made Jacob cringe every day as he drove past. On this day, however, he read the sign and inched his foot off the accelerator before finally resting it firmly on the brake pedal.

Emily would probably like some flowers, he thought. Images of pencil-breasts floated about his brain, trying desperately to take on flesh.

He turned onto the gravel parking lot and his truck buckled and shook as the tires passed over a field of potholes. "Jesus Christ!" he shouted as his head collided against the steering wheel. He slammed on the breaks and threw his hand up to his swelling forehead. He could feel the bump growing larger by the second. "Shit," he muttered.

Though it sat in the direct center of the lot, Jacob threw the truck into park and scrambled out of the seat onto the dusty ground. He stared at his reflection in the side mirror, and realized the bump wasn't *really* all that bad. He was more concerned about the cut on his forehead. Sometimes these things got infected and they'd have to take half your face off just to stem it. One could never be too careful.

Through the glass door of the store, he could see an elderly woman watching him through pink eye glasses. Feeling embarrassed, he briefly considered getting back in the truck and driving away, but that would just look more ridiculous. He decided to do the normal thing and go inside. He needed ointment for the swelling anyway, and Emily would still like those flowers.

"G'morning!" he shouted cheerily as he walked through the door of the store, the bell tinkling above him.

"Afternoon, you mean," the pink-glassed lady answered from behind the counter to his left.

"Yes, erm, afternoon," Jacob said bashfully, and quickly ducked into one of the low-standing aisles.

"These would be just perfect for dear, sweet Emily," Bill said.

Jacob turned and saw him burying his tiny, black body into a large red rose. "This is magnificent," Bill sighed, twitching this way and that like a minuscule bumble bee. "So soft. So warm."

"Stop that," Jacob said, snatching the whole bundle of twelve. There was something about Bill's movements that he didn't like. He stared at the flowers. Maybe it was too much—too romantic.

"It's perfect," Bill said, flying out from the rose and landing on a travel-size bag of potato chips that hung on a hook nearby. "Classy. Women appreciate class."

Jacob thought of Humphrey Bogart, and knew that Bill was right.

"You might want to get something for your head as well," said the fly. "It's beginning to swell."

Jacob had nearly forgotten.

At the checkout counter, laden with a dozen roses wrapped in plastic and a bottle of some pink ointment with a giant red cross on it which assured him that it would get the job done, Jacob smiled awkwardly to the stone-faced elderly woman with the pink glasses. She stared coldly back, her eyes magnified ridiculously through the lenses. He tried desperately to think of something to say to her, but the only thing that came to him was the awful state of the parking lot.

"Been awhile since the outside's been paved, huh?" he said.

The woman stared, and said, "Is that all?"

"What?" Jacob stammered before looking down at the items he had laid on the counter. "Oh, yes. This is it."

The woman huffed and brought out the portable scanner, ringing both items up with a distinctive *deet deet*.

"This darn thing," the woman said, *deeting* the barcode on the bag of flowers over and over again each time the computer failed to pick it up. *Deet deet deet.*

She kept *deeting*, and Jacob noticed Bill was buzzing just beyond his ear canal—buzzing in the same maddening pattern as the woman's *deeting*. His tiny wings were taking on the sound even, and Jacob could feel his blood pressure rising. He could feel the walls of his arteries constricting, his heart palpitating, trying in vain to pump his thick blood through all of his extremities. It was getting caught somewhere near his neck, choking off his brain, and he knew he'd be dead in only a few minutes if she didn't shut right the hell up.

"Jesus Christ!" Jacob shouted, snatching the scanner from her. In one swift motion, he sent it flying right into the old woman's cold, blank face; the collision forcing lines resembling a smile and making up for the one she had failed to give him before when he had told her "G'morning!"

She let out a ragged cry and Jacob pounded her again, a bit harder this time. She was quiet after that, lying down on the floor. The only sounds were her shallow breathing and a slight whimper.

"God, I was beginning to tire of that one," Bill said, still hovering next to Jacob's ear. "Human beings who are completely incapable of basic courtesy really make my blood boil."

"Jesus," Jacob muttered. "What did I—"

"Never mind that," Bill said. "Emily works the morning shift, and it's nearly one o'clock already. She only has another hour. We must get moving!"

Bill took off, and Jacob lost sight of him as he flew against a black poster promoting energy drinks that sat near the register. The woman's breathing had grown louder, and Jacob hurried out of the store to his truck. As he drove away, he felt the urge to glance back towards the store, but he kept his gaze fixed forward, and resisted the temptation to look up into his rearview mirror.

4.

By the time he arrived at the factory, Jacob could tell that the peak of the day had passed. The smokestacks seemed to dispatch a lighter shade of darkness, lazily casting the factory's repugnance up into the sky, and the wrens roosting in the building's cracks and crevices let out only the quietest of calls. The clouds slunk by dreamily, morphing into any of a number of nameless, indiscernible shapes that Jacob swore were fluffy rabbits. His neck was craned upwards towards a particularly fluffy one as he passed through the large, metal double-doors of the factory and collided into Mr. Jay's enormous belly.

"Late, Kingsley," Mr. Jay said, his lips thin and sinking into his jaw. He pointed accusingly at the lone unbuttoned button in Jacob's work shirt, adopting it as the literal and physical manifestation of his employee's incompetence. "Late. Late. Late!"

"I'm sorry," Jacob said simply. He brushed past Mr. Jay and took off to his locker, keeping a brisk pace and doing his best to keep the flowers tucked under his arm from view.

He passed the whirring machines and could practically feel the judgmental glances of everyone in the massive workroom bearing down upon the loose skin of his neck. He hoped that Emily's wasn't among them, but he figured it probably was. He thought about looking up from his feet to check, but it was better not knowing. On second thought, she was a sweet girl. She wouldn't look at him like that. She was probably looking at all of the other, judging eyes and upbraiding them for their meanness. She was on his side, and that was an encouraging thought.

His feet collided against metal and Jacob looked up, noticing that he had arrived at the row of lockers in the break room. He quickly shoved the flowers into his own, and scrounged about inside for the long-discarded lock, digging through piles of loose notebook paper, many of them bearing images of breasts and female genitalia with the name "Emily" peppered in every now and then.

"Don't put them in there. They'll be crushed," Bill said, landing gently on one of the thick, dark hairs of Jacob's arm.

Jacob ignored him, but he folded a portion of the papers neatly and placed them on the floor of the locker to make a safe bed for the roses.

"Fuck off, Jack. You know you haven't seen a pussy in weeks," Emily's lovely voice rang out as she and a crowd of male admirers, first-shift people, stormed into the break room. Jacob quickly slammed the door of his locker closed.

"Decided to show up?" Mark Benjamin said, slapping Jacob on the shoulder with a laugh. Jacob flinched with surprise.

Mark Benjamin was an ass. His hair was buzzed along the side and the back, but kept long on the top, cascading down into his eyebrows in long, greasy strips that would bounce up and down to his shrill cackle of a laugh. His face was heavily scarred from an obviously pimpled youth, and his eyes seemed incredibly small for his head. He looked like a rat, and Jacob knew that he was. Physiognomy never lied. His arms were blighted with ancient tattoos, their lines smudged and faded. Jacob stared at these as Mark stood close by. It was better than looking at his snide little smile.

"Better late than never, I guess, huh?" Mark said in a much colder tone. "Jay had me running all over the damn place covering your ass, and you just mosey on in here."

"I'm sorry," Jacob said simply.

Mark scoffed and went to his locker at the end of the row. Emily went to the time clock at the wall, and the rest of her posse drifted away.

"Now's your chance," Bill said.

"No, not with Mark here," Jacob replied.

"What?" Emily said suddenly.

"Do it," Bill said, lifting off his hairy perch and buzzing beside Jacob's ear. "She's asking for it. Look at her."

There she was, standing by the time clock with her pinkish lips curled slightly in an inquisitive expression. "Did you say something?" she asked.

"I did," Jacob said slowly, immobile.

"Give them to her," Bill whispered. "Don't leave her standing there."

I can't, Jacob thought. *I'll do it later—when Mark isn't here.*

"There may not be a later," Bill said. "*Carpe diem*, friend. Do it."

The electronic time clock chimed and Emily began to walk towards the door.

"She's leaving. You're mucking this up," Bill snarled.

Mark laughed over by his locker. "Oh my God, Emily, you have to see this," he said, looking at a magazine he had retrieved.

"Emily!" Jacob shouted, and she turned around in surprise. He looked down and saw that he was grasping the roses in his fist with an iron grip, his knuckles turning white.

"Holy shit!" Mark laughed, staring wide eyed at the scene and grinning his stupid grin. Hearing his exclamation, Emily's posse filed back into the room and stared at Jacob curiously. "Looks like you've got yourself a boyfriend, Em."

"Shut up, Mark," Emily said, regaining her composure.

Jacob forced tunnel vision upon himself, staring only at Emily. However, his nervousness forbade him to keep eye contact with her and his gaze descended to her chest. "Here," he mumbled as he extended the roses towards her.

His arm lingered, wavering in the air. The laughter of Mark and the posse quieted into silence.

They waited with eyes wide in expectation.

Emily slowly took the roses and let her laden arm fall limp at her side. "What's this supposed to be for?"

Bill's tiny wings flapped sporadically, just outside Jacob's ear. "They're for you," Jacob said.

"Why?"

A slight chuckle escaped Mark's curling lips, and it sounded too much like a *deet*. It made the thick blood fly through Jacob's veins, congealing, once again, at the base of his skull. "If something is fucking funny to you, why don't you let me in on it!" Jacob shouted, angling his head ever so slightly towards Mark.

"Shit, man," Mark smirked, nervously looking at the posse, gauging their reactions. They would decide whether Jacob Kingsley received a laugh or a pounding. Their faces were blank; no help there. "What's eating you, Jacob?" Mark said as he walked closer.

"Stay away from me!" Jacob shouted, extending his arm and pointing a shaky index finger in Mark's direction.

"Jeez. You need to take a break. Have a breather." Mark pulled one of the small metal chairs out from a nearby table. "Have a seat. Chill out."

Jacob looked around as if he was becoming aware of his surroundings for the first time, and slowly sat down. He took a deep breath. "I was hoping, Emily—" he began.

"Give it a rest, man," Mark said, laughing to himself.

"I was hoping, Emily, that you would do me the honor of taking you to dinner," Jacob said, much louder. "Maybe tomorrow night?"

Mark's eyes widened, and he stared at Emily knowingly as the smirk returned to his face.

"Classy, Jacob. Perfect and classy," Bill said.

Emily looked to the posse, to Mark, and finally rested her gaze on Jacob, but for only a fleeting moment. "The flowers are very nice," she said.

"I picked them out myself," Jacob smiled.

"I'm sure you did," she answered. "I'll—I'll go out to dinner with you."

Jacob smiled, too delighted to respond. He barely noticed as she hastily quit the room with Mark and the posse at her heels. As the door to the break room shut, he could hear Mark and the posse's loud laughter echoing off the walls of the adjacent room. Emily's sweet, delicate voice rose above it all, doubtlessly chastising them for being so cruel to her Jacob.

5.

Needless to say, Jacob didn't have the capacity to perform work that afternoon. He was too busy wondering what sweet delicacies Emily kept under her factory-provided work attire, knowing that, soon, he wouldn't have to wonder. It would be just like the first date he had gone on with Maddy, he was sure of it: Howie's Pizza Barn for their all-you-can-eat special, followed by a trip to the cinema to see *Murderblast 4: The Reckoning*. The unbridled adrenaline of the picture, and the caffeine from the gallon-sized sodas would get both their bloods pumping. They would explode later in the evening with unbridled sexual contact after shot-gunning a few beers while playing *Call of Violence* on Game-Box. It was a system for the perfect date, and Jacob had seen it in action. He knew it worked. *Murderblast 8* wasn't due in theaters till later in the year, but that was no matter. He'd find a fitting cinematic substitute.

"I hear *Escape from Gun Island* is particularly thrilling," Bill said as Jacob leaned up against his machine.

Jacob had heard the same, but he wasn't going to admit it to Bill. He was still trying not to talk to him too much. His very existence was disturbing.

"By the way—I'm proud of you, Jacob," Bill said, buzzing tenderly as he landed on the shoulder of Jacob's work shirt. "You've shown some real motivation. You went out there, got what you wanted, showed some initiative. And you reaped the rewards… despite the desperate machinations of that bastard, Mark Benjamin. You should have pounded his skinny face right in. I don't understand how he thinks he can sit there smirking like that. What right has he to smirk? He's a grease monkey—just like his father before him, and *his* father before *him*. He hasn't worked at a prestigious law firm like you. He hasn't held the kind of responsibility you have, shown the kind of initiative you have!"

Jacob found Bill's delivery a little jarring, but he had to admit that his words were undeniably true. "You're right, Bill. Damn right."

"Damn right I'm damn right!" Bill said. "You're a god to that miserable whelp, and he—he's a blasphemer! He should be put in his place one of these days."

Jacob nodded, and went back to daydreaming.

Five o'clock came quickly—much quicker than Jacob had anticipated. It seemed that he had only done a half-day's work, but he wasn't one to complain about a good thing. He clocked out and passed Mr. Jay on his way out the door just like everyone else, though he was puzzled by the man's sour expression seemingly aimed at him.

As he drove his truck down Grissom Street and passed the mom and pop store, he thought he saw two police cars parked in the field of potholes, their lights flashing in the gathering haze. The sight alarmed him, and he quickly glanced up into his rearview mirror. He realized he was mistaken. There was no one. The lights inside the store were out, and the spotlight that usually shined upon the large sign on the roof was dark as well. The owners must have closed up early.

A few minutes later, Jacob pulled into the driveway of his home and killed the engine. For a moment, he sat quietly in the darkened truck. So much had happened to him in the course of only a few hours, and he needed to soak it in a bit. He had won Emily Grainger. The knowledge was almost too much for him, and he felt like he would explode. *If only Maddy could see me now,* he thought. *Her whole reason for leaving me, blown out of the water! Look at Jacob Kingsley achieve now!*

He could not stem the growing smile that stretched across his face as he left the truck. His steps were more like skips as he walked up to his front door and put his key in the lock. There really was no reason why he *couldn't* tell Maddy about Emily. As he walked inside the house and hit the light in the foyer, the idea had grown immensely more enticing. He wouldn't call her, he'd text her. That was better—more aloof. He wouldn't look desperate to talk to her. Plus, he could add a picture of Emily so that she'd know the kind of action her dear, stupid, unmotivated ex was getting. That would set her off. That would get her stupid sideways ponytail spinning.

He didn't have one on his phone, but could procure a photograph easily enough. Emily was on all the social sites. He typed her name into the tiny search bar on his laptop from the grease-stained couch in the living room and took in the familiar sight of her 753 profile pictures once the page loaded. Jacob knew them all by heart, and he scanned through them lovingly, searching for just the right one to set Maddy off.

"They're missing a certain something, don't you think?" Bill said, resting gently on the open screen of the laptop.

"I think they're wonderful," Jacob said, staring longingly at one of Emily in her backyard. Her lips were pinker than they usually were.

"They're great. Don't get me wrong," Bill sighed, "but I don't think they'll show Madeline what an ass she's been—how wrong she was about you."

"What do you mean?"

"We need a little more pizazz. There's got to be one in there more glamorous than these casual shots."

Even though he had them all memorized, Jacob went through all the photos again.

"Anything in a bikini?" Bill asked.

"Nah. I guess she's the bashful sort," Jacob replied, finding himself strangely aroused.

"Damn. Well, we'll just have to make do."

In a flash, an image of a busty nude blonde woman lying spread-eagle on the satin sheets of a queen-sized bed appeared on the laptop screen. Jacob had seen it before. It was one of a numberless collection of images he had stored in a folder on his desktop innocuously labeled, "Scrapbooking."

"What am I supposed to do with this?" Jacob asked.

In a second flash, his photo-editing software opened in a new window. "Use the one where she's had a little too much at that tailgating party," Bill said. "For whatever reason, 'just north of tipsy' looks like 'smoldering sex-goddess' on some women."

"Wait, what do you want me to do?" Jacob said.

In a third flash, a second image was pulled up. This was an ancient one of Maddy. Jacob's heart began beating hard, and his palms grew sweaty. It was an image he had saved for years: the first nude she had ever sent him. It was too precious to keep with the smut in "Scrapbooking." It had its own folder, "New Folder." He hadn't even named it. There weren't words adequate enough. It was sent to him back when they were both in high school. The bathroom wall behind her perky breasts was the red and gold of the Frederick Badgers. When he had received the photo, he felt light and fuzzy and thanked her profusely despite her assurances that she wanted to send it of her own loving volition. He spent the rest of the period glancing at it under his desk.

When he had gotten home, he rushed straight to his room and uploaded it to his computer. Once blown up on his full-sized monitor, he noticed that the picture was grainy, and the dim lighting of the bathroom made Maddy's smiling face white as a ghost's. Until two o'clock in the morning, he lovingly edited it in his photo-editing software, correcting the colors, lighting, and bringing the image to a new peak of perfection. He tried to make it look less like a cheap flip-phone photo. He wanted the real thing.

He showed the completed product to Maddy the next day in the halls after second period. She was touched, kissed him—his first kiss. She was his girlfriend by the time the bell rang.

"You know what to do. You've done it before," Bill said, breaking Jacob from his stupor. "Work the software. Give Emily here a little oomph."

There was a moment—but only a moment—that Jacob hesitated, his cursor hovering in the photo-editing program. He and Maddy had had good times, but that only made her rejection of him—her utter and complete betrayal of the man who had given her so much—all the more painful. Jacob opened up the picture of Emily at the tailgating party (he knew exactly where it was) and ripped her intoxicated head right off her body. He opened up the image of the spread-eagled porn star (he thought her name was Vickie Vixxen, but he couldn't be sure) and pasted Emily's head on top of hers. Changing the color of the hair and blending the skin tones together was easy enough, and Jacob thought the finished product looked pretty good.

Bill gasped. "It's perfect."

To inspect the fine details, Jacob printed the picture out. When the printer's loud churning ceased, he grabbed the image and found it flawless—by far, his finest work. Maddy would be furious. Doubtlessly she would be so filled with envy that she would search the social sites in a desperate attempt to prove Jacob's claim false, but she'd only find that the surreally sexual body she was so jealous of matched the face of Emily Grainger, Jacob Kingsley's beloved girlfriend, perfectly. He returned to his laptop and downloaded the picture onto his phone. Everything was ready, now.

His stubby thumbs flew across the tiny keyboard on his phone, and he typed out a message he hoped would illicit an immense emotional response from Maddy. He carefully constructed each sentence, and, when he had finished, he pushed back into the sinking couch cushions and painstakingly reviewed his work.

Hey, Maddy. I'm doing fantastic. Got a good job down here, and I'm dating a gorgeous girl (See attached photo). She's a Brazilian model. Only part, of course (Brazilian, not model. She models full-time and goes to New York and Seattle and LA a lot).

He smiled when he reached the end of his sixth reading, and was about to hit "Send" when he added, as an afterthought:

Hope you're doing okay.

This final addendum would showcase his sensitive side, thus making Maddy not only jealous of the beauty of his new girlfriend, but of the loving, tender care she was receiving.

"Great addition," Bill said, landing on an empty beer bottle by the couch.

"This will get her rolling," Jacob smiled as he emphatically pressed the "Send" button. The tiny hourglass appeared in the screen, followed by the confirmation, "Sent!" Jacob's smile abruptly turned. He had forgotten to attach the picture!

"Quick! We can't have her thinking you're a fuck up. I doubt she'd think you're successful—motivated—if you forgot to send the damned attachment!" Bill shouted, buzzing furiously about the phone inches from Jacob's face.

Jacob squinted, trying to peer past the darting black body that blocked his view of the phone. "I got it. I got it," he said, attaching the photo to a new message.

Here's the picture. I delayed its sending by a few seconds for dramatic effect. I think you'll agree that it's worth it.

"Send it!" Bill screamed, and Jacob pushed the "Send" button again. "Good," Bill huffed. "Good. Well done." His wings moved slowly, and he drifted off towards the bedroom, breathing rapidly and heavily.

Jacob's confidence dissipated with each second void of Maddy's reply. Maybe she wouldn't buy it. Maybe she could tell the picture was a forgery—but she was never very good with computers. She preferred books—dry, boring books thousands of pages long about pastoral English nobility, or denizens of St. Petersburg. Those were the kinds of things she liked. Jacob remembered, and a short burst of air escaped his lips in a scoff. She was an idiot—too wrapped up in her reading to actually engage with reality, and too busy chasing imaginary ideals to see that she had a pretty good life with him. He had taken care of her, hadn't he?

He stood up from the couch, suddenly thirsty for a beer. Maddy's scrunched up nose, inches from the worn pages of a copy of *The Brothers Karamazov*, flooded his memory. It twitched slightly as she turned the page, her eyes darting rapidly as she took in every word.

"How can you read that stuff?" Jacob said, shouting over the explosions and gunshots of *Call of Violence* as his fingers pounded the controller.

"I like it," she replied, not moving her eyes from the page. "It's really good, Jake. You should give it a chance."

"You know, we used to play this game together," Jacob said. "Do you remember that? Do you want me to plug in another controller?"

"No, I'm good."

"What do you mean? You're good?" he shouted, rising angrily to his feet and slamming the controller down.

"Gosh, calm down! What's your problem?" she shouted, contorting her face in a look of surprise and repulsion.

"You know exactly what my problem is!" He walked over to her chair and the cap on the beer in his hand was open and the memory was pushed away as the frothy liquid slid down his throat.

His phone vibrated loudly from the couch in a deep *vrrr vrrr*. Slowly, he walked to it and stared speechless at the glowing display. He had long ago deleted Maddy from his phone, but he had the number memorized.

"Answer it," Bill said, appearing suddenly on his shoulder. Jacob hadn't heard him approach.

"I texted her. I don't want to talk," Jacob replied.

Bill flew off his shoulder and touched down hard on the green answer button.

"Hello? Jake?" Maddy's voice called out, soft and pretty from the phone's tiny speaker. "Jake, you there?"

"Yes, yes, I'm here!" Jacob shouted, quickly snatching the phone off the couch and bringing it to his ear.

"Hey," she said, her voice sounding sadder than it was before. "I just got your text."

"Yeah," Jacob said.

"What was that about? Are you okay?"

"Yeah. I'm fine. I just wanted you to know that I'm perfectly fine. I'm doing great. Did you see my new girlfriend?"

"Yeah, I did. I'm happy for you."

This wasn't the kind of reply he wanted. He had to bring it up a notch. He had to increase the pressure. "I found a good job."

"Yeah? Where? Do you like it better than dad's law office? I know you said you hated the internship there."

"I'm a factory manager. Got the whole place to myself. Yeah, it's way better."

"I'm glad to hear it, Jake."

Now what, he thought. "How're you doing these days? Still living with your boss?" He tried to keep the venom out of his voice, but it found its way in anyway.

"I told you," Maddy sighed. "I was living with Christie. The fact that her dad was my office manager was just a coincidence. He never gave me any special treatment. He barely said a word to me."

"Was?"

"Huh?"

"You said that he was your office manager."

"Oh, yeah. I'm working in New York. I got a job at that publishing company I was telling you about. It's just copy editing. I don't have any real decision-making there, but it's a start."

The excitement in her voice badly stung. "I'd probably send out a few applications somewhere else," he said. "No one reads books anymore. It's all digital with e-books and stuff."

"People still like books," she said simply.

"I don't like them."

"You're not the only person in the world, Jake."

They said nothing for a few short, maddening moments. Jacob could feel the old blood coming on again.

"What a joke," Bill said. "She thinks she's so much better than everyone else."

"Jake, are you there?"

"Her reaction to your life finally looking up is, 'Jakey, you okay? You feeling alright?' Disgusting."

"Jake?"

"Uh…"

"She'll never learn. I don't know why you waste your time on such human filth."

"Are you there?"

Jacob's thumb slammed onto the red "End" button and he hung up. He casually threw the phone back onto the couch and stared at the surprisingly empty bottle in his other hand. There were only a few drops left. He drained them as he walked back into the kitchen for another.

6.

Jacob stayed awake in a fog of television and GameBox until around two in the morning, when he lazily parted the sea of empty beer cans and stomped into the bedroom. He didn't bother brushing his teeth or even undressing. He simply flopped down onto the yellowed sheets of his bed and smiled. Tomorrow was the day, and, tomorrow night, Emily would be beside him in his bed—he just knew it. He threw his arm out from where it was pinned under his belly and pretended like he was grabbing her sides, raking her towards himself.

He dreamt that he was back in his childhood home in Connecticut. He was sitting Indian-style on the shag carpet with two of his older sister's Barbie dolls in his hands—a brunette and a blonde. He remembered them well. A pair of scissors sat nearby, and the blonde he held in his right hand had her nose, ear, and half her face missing. Shreds of plastic were strewn about the floor. He rotated the mangled doll, examining his work on all sides, and heard a small voice. It sounded a little like Natalie, but she had gone to her piano lesson. It grew steadily louder and he realized it was coming from the newly-created cavity inside the doll's head.

He held it up to his eyes and peered inside. It was dark—too dark. It was inky black, and the plastic sides of the doll's head which Jacob knew must exist weren't visible. Only the darkness.

"Thanks for the flowers, Jake," the voice said, sounding like a mixture of both Maddy and Emily now. The realization scared him, and he quickly lurched backward and threw the doll onto the ground. Maddy's dark-green eye set in the still-intact side of the doll's face stared back at him, or was it Emily's blue? It seemed to change right in front of him.

A noise outside—distant at first, but growing steadily. It was a thump followed by a sound of twisting metal or springs. It filled Jacob with dread, but he knew he had to look. He left the doll and rose to his feet, inching closer to the open window past his sister's canopied princess bed. As he arrived at the window, he felt the warm summer breeze blow through his hair. It was much more pleasant than Arizona.

He turned towards the sound, frightened of what he might see. There was nothing at first, but, slowly, a figure rounded the turn and started down Barrow Lane. It was bouncing up and down smoothly, and the only thing Jacob could think of was a giant kangaroo. As the figure approached, he noticed that its pigment was lighter than a kangaroo's, and that it had human breasts.

"Hey, Jake!" the naked woman waved, bouncing up and down on her pogo stick, her face looking flushed and tired—but still smiling.

Jacob waved cautiously back, slightly put off by the way the woman's face changed from Maddy to Emily, and even sometimes to Katie Daran, a girl who used to live next door to him that he hadn't thought of in years. He watched bemusedly as she bounced by his window, panting and huffing, and then the *deeting* began.

The first sensation was that his pants were wet, and the second was that the alarm clock on his night stand was sounding wildly. As his mind caught up with his body however, he realized that the noises were knocks from his front door. He quickly undressed and tossed his soiled boxers into the sink in the bathroom. He put on a new set, and also his jeans and white t-shirt before walking slowly to the door, checking his breath by breathing into his hand and smelling. It was alright.

The knocks grew louder, and, Jacob thought, more desperate. They annoyed him. "I'm coming," he shouted, only a few feet from the door. "Jesus Christ."

He opened it to find Mark Benjamin standing on his doorstep.

"What the hell is *he* doing here?" Bill said, appearing from somewhere in the kitchen and buzzing angrily about Jacob's ear.

"Hey, Jacob," Mark said nervously—with that stupid smirk.

"Hey," Jacob returned, equally nervous.

"Do you mind if I come in?"

"Aren't you supposed to be at the factory?"

Mark laughed a little. "It's Saturday."

"Oh," Jacob said, nodding his head rapidly up and down.

Mark walked inside and Jacob skirted out of the way. Bill's buzzing was incredibly loud as he flew about the room. Jacob hadn't remembered it ever being so loud.

Mark stood awkwardly between the card table in the dining room and the sea of empty beer bottles by the couch in the living room, nervously cupping and rubbing his calloused hands together. "Hey, so, uh, I wanted to talk to you about Emily," he said.

"Would you like something to drink, a beer maybe, unless it's too early?" Jacob chimed in, and looked at the digital clock on the floor by the television. It read only eleven. "Probably too early. Coffee then?"

"Sure, sure," Mark replied. As Jacob went into the kitchen, Mark began speaking rapidly. "Hey, so I'm here on behalf of Emily, okay?"

"Okay," Jacob said as he put a new filter into the coffee pot.

"Yeah, so, uh, she was too embarrassed to tell you, so she made me—"

"Hungry?" Jacob called out cheerily. "Did you get anything for breakfast?"

"Yeah, I'm good. Thanks," Mark said.

"Do you mind if I put something on?"

"No, no. It's your house, man."

Jacob put all of the burners onto their highest level and put a skillet on top of each. In the first he put three strips of bacon. In the second, he put four sausages, and, in the third and fourth, he put two eggs. He added a little bit of olive oil in each dish, not because he liked the flavor, but because he hoped to make them sizzle as loud as they possibly could—anything to drown out Mark Benjamin's idiotic drones.

"Anyways, she wanted me to pay you a visit," Mark began again. He was persistent.

"I'm sorry, I can't hear you!" Jacob called out, pleased at the loud sizzling that had begun to take over his kitchen.

"I said, she wanted me to—"

"I still can't hear. I'm sorry!"

"Okay, I'll just wait then," Mark said, sitting down at the single place at the card table.

It was only a matter of time now. Jacob's bacon had already crisped and was on the verge of burning. His eggs had been bubbling needlessly on one side for about an eternity, and the sausage had begun to smoke. He needed more food.

"You've got the meat and the eggs," Bill said, "but you still don't have a complete breakfast. Where's the vitamin C or the calcium? Those should give us a little more time."

"Right," Jacob exclaimed, delighted as he rushed to the refrigerator and brought out two large grapefruits. He was lucky he had them, but a well-stocked fridge was one of the many things he took pride in.

"What'd you say?" Mark said from the card table.

"Nothing. I can't hear you!" Jacob shouted back.

He cut up the grapefruit and carefully, delicately arranged it on a paper plate.

"It needs a garnish," Bill said.

"Yeah, but what?" Jacob answered.

"Did you say something?" Mark shouted from the other room.

"I don't know," Bill sighed. "Check the fridge."

Jacob rushed back to the fridge and found a package of blueberries. They would be perfect to offset the deep reds of the grapefruit. He took a handful and washed them carefully under running water, and then dumped them in the middle of the ring of grapefruit slices he had made.

"Calcium!" Bill reprimanded.

Jacob nodded and returned, once again, to the fridge. He took out the gallon of milk and poured himself a large glass. He removed the meats and eggs from the skillet and put them on a plate, but left the grease to burn and sizzle on the high stove. He sighed, took his first bite of burnt-to-a-crisp bacon, and realized that Mark was standing less than two feet from him, leaned up against the counter opposite the fridge.

"So, like I was going to say, Emily can't make the date tonight," he said suddenly. "She just doesn't see you that way."

Jacob said nothing, and stared as Bill flew loudly about his head.

"I hope you're not too upset, Jake. She would have told you herself, but she didn't want to see you upset."

"I'm not upset."

"Okay. Okay, I'm glad," Mark said, beginning to smirk. "But, man, you had to know we were going out. We didn't make a point of hiding it. I thought everybody knew!"

Somewhere, in some faraway exotic place, a *deet*, a loud, thunderous *deet* was starting up, and Jacob could hear its every peal. It grew in volume, and began to vibrate the appliances in the kitchen.

"You had to know, Jake, that I'm stuffing Emily every night!" Mark was saying, his smirk growing wider. "You had to know that she's begging for me to give it to her, bent over, smiling the whole time."

The *deet* was sending cracks down the walls. Jacob could see them growing wider as Mark ran his mouth.

"She loves it, man. She's a fire in bed, and she'll do anything I say." Mark's smirk had somehow reached beyond the confines of his head, and was stretching his pock-marked face from wall to wall.

The *deet* sent a huge crack along the floor.

"You had to know that I fuck her every night, and she laughs whenever I bring up your name," Mark said, before a knife was plunged into his throat, making all his words only drowned gurgles.

The cracks and the *deets* were gone, and Mark fell to the floor as blood spurted out of his neck. He gasped, fighting to keep what little life still remained within him, and then his head fell face down as his eyes rolled back. Jacob looked down to his hand—to the bloody knife in his hand—and let out a gasp.

"Finally, a little quiet," Bill said.

7.

Detective Robert Killian shot out of bed with a start, sweat dripping from his forehead and his normally steady pulse registering at what he figured to be around the 120 mark. *Too fast for a man who's just woken up,* he thought. It was normal for him to get up to 120, or even 140, but only during his morning three-mile run around the development or his afternoon squats with the 10lb kettlebell he kept under his desk in the office—never right after waking up in the morning. Something was amiss. The universe was trying to tell him something.

He jumped to his feet and did his normal stretching regimen. He bent down and touched his toes, holding the position until he could feel the burn in his legs, and then reached up and extended his arms towards the ceiling as he stood on his tip toes. He could feel the slothful immobility of the night leaving his body, and he felt his chi expanding. With such strange purpose hanging over his head, he knew he'd have to spend extra time in his pre-breakfast meditation. But there was time for that. He turned to his breathing exercises, picturing himself as the large forward sail of a seventeenth century English Merchantman—receiving the wind when it came, and falling down flat as it left.

When he had finished, he walked to the bathroom and flipped the light on. He brought out the white kitchen timer he kept in the drawer and set it for exactly two minutes and fifteen seconds. Two minutes was the norm, but Robert figured that the extra fifteen seconds couldn't hurt. He brought out his toothbrush from the plastic zip-bag that sat next to the timer, turned the faucet over the sink, and dipped the brush into the water before putting on a pea-sized drop of toothpaste. He shut the water off and started the timer.

When it sounded, he rinsed out his mouth and thoroughly rinsed his toothbrush before unfolding one of the towels on the counter and thoroughly drying the bristles. He held the brush up to the light, looking for any signs of wetness. It wasn't worth the chance of mildew. Satisfied, he returned the brush to the zip-bag and rinsed his mouth out with the mouthwash his dentist had recommended. Robert had read an article in *The Natural Man* that said Kreest Komplete worked a little better, so he rinsed with that once he had finished. It couldn't hurt. Now he needed his word.

He walked over to his standing-desk in the living room and stood in front of his computer. He brought out the timer in the desk drawer and set it for five minutes. The internet could be an alluring place, and he didn't want to stare at a screen for too long. Screens were terrible on the eyes. He went to masterjim.com and hit the flashing yellow button on the page for his word of the day. The screen turned white while the new page was loaded. When it finally appeared, Robert had to fight to keep his inner peace. Confusion began to sift down from his conscious mind. The word was strawberry.

Strawberry? What the fuck am I supposed to do with strawberry? his flesh said, but he quieted it. There had to be something in it. There had to be something about a strawberry that unlocked the key to the rude awakening he had received. Fate had dealt him "strawberry" and he would acquiesce to her demands.

He flipped on his white noise machine and sat cross-legged in the middle of the floor. He tried to drown out the sound of the neighborhood children playing in their yards—the sound of their laughter, the barking of their dogs. It wasn't working so well, so he turned up the volume on the machine. Loud buzzing filled the room and he closed his eyes, sinking into his transcendental state.

"Strawberry," he whispered, his lips barely moving. He thought of how the word bounced around inside his mouth and slid off his tongue. "Strawberry."

There had to be an answer—a clue. There had to be something in "strawberry" that could explain what the universe was trying to tell him. There had to be something.

"Strawberry. Strawberry…"

8.

Jacob's vision was blurred, and his hands shook wildly. All he saw were fragments and mismatched colors. Tan, Blue, Red.

"Jesus Christ," he was saying—over and over again.

"Get a grip on yourself," Bill said casually.

"Jesus Christ."

"You need to calm down."

"Jesus—"

"Calm the fuck down!" Bill shouted, flying angrily down onto Mark's broken and bloody corpse. "Freaking out isn't going to help the situation, now. We need to be calm—collected—and handle this."

Jacob could barely hear what Bill was saying. The only sound was the sound of his heart pounding mercilessly in his ears. It thumped against his skull, morphing into the sound of fists colliding against his large body. They were the fists of the arresting police officers, the inmates he shared a cell with, but also the fists of his dad, black and greasy from a day of working at Mr. Drake's auto shop, and those of his mother—and Maddy. They were pounding him mercilessly as he writhed on the dirty cell floor and screamed.

"Do you hear me?" Bill shouted, and the words broke through.

"What?" Jacob panted.

"I asked if you have a sledge hammer."

"Yeah, I think so."

"Good, go get it."

Jacob ran through the kitchen to the hallway, and opened the door to the garage. In the corner, sat the sledgehammer that was a piece of the toolset the landlord had left for the house's renters. He had never used any of the tools before, but he was thankful they were there now. Evidently, he needed them. He wasn't sure why, but Bill had a plan.

With the sledgehammer in tow, he walked back into the house and almost retched as he stepped into the kitchen. It was like seeing the scene for the first time.

"Don't be such a child," Bill scolded. "Take the hammer and knock out the wall behind your closet."

"What?"

"Just do it."

Jacob nodded and walked to the bedroom. He parted the few nice clothes he had on hangers and took the hammer to the wall. He had expected the task to be much more difficult than it was, and soon the wall was down, with large, white chunks of dry-wall clinging to the carpet and dust floating idly in the air.

"Come over here and help me with this," Bill called suddenly. His voice sounded muffled and echoed.

Jacob followed it, and found Mark lying on the rug in the bathroom next to the tub. Bill's six tiny feet clung to Mark's nose, and his wings moved rapidly. "Can you help, here?" Bill asked.

"How did you get him all the way over there in the first place?"

"Never mind. Just help me get him in."

Jacob cringed and closed his eyes as he held Mark underneath his arms. He could feel the blood on his hands, but he ignored it and heaved the body up and into the tub. It felt lighter than he thought it would, and Bill's wings were moving furiously.

Jacob quickly opened his eyes and turned away, relieved that the task was done. "So, what now?"

"Do you have a hand saw?" Bill asked.

The question made Jacob's heart jump. "Why?"

"We need to make him more manageable."

Jacob began to sweat. "No, no, I can't do that. Can't we just bury him somewhere?"

"No, that's absolutely out of the question. Get the saw."

"What? Why?"

"Too many variables—animals, rain, neighbors. There's no way to ensure that the body will remain hidden."

"We can keep a close eye on it. He's not going anywhere. It's not like he'll just get up and walk away!"

Bill issued a stern buzz, flew slowly off of Mark

in the tub, and rested on the bathroom counter, leaving small specks of red as he cleaned his feet. "Jacob," he said, "get the saw."

Jacob walked back to the garage. He knew where the saw was. He had seen it every day, hanging on a peg by the garage door. He took it off and returned to the bathroom, staring at the saw's teeth and imagining them cutting through muscle and bone.

"I can't do this," he stammered as he returned. "I can't."

Bill flew onto his shoulder. "He needs to be smaller. He won't fit in the wall this way, and, compartmentalized, he'll break down faster."

"Okay," Jacob said, though he was barely aware of it.

He got down on one knee and lifted up Mark's thigh. He placed the teeth down on the corpse's flesh, and felt liquid rise to his throat.

"I can't do this. I can't fucking do this."

"Fine," Bill said.

"What—what do you mean?"

"That's fine. I'll do it, then."

"You'll do it? How?"

"Just go to the hardware store and get me a few things. I made a list. It's on the counter in the kitchen."

Jacob walked quickly to the kitchen, amazed at how a creature with no hands or fingers could somehow write a note. To his surprise, the linoleum floor was completely clean. Not a drop of red, and it smelled kind of lemony. As Jacob took the note off the counter, he cast a nervous glance in the direction of the bathroom… and heard the crunch of the saw moving back and forth.

9.

The doors slid open and wobbled noisily in their tracks as Jacob walked inside Grace Hardware N' Home Supplies. The drive over had been a blur, and he had thought he'd seen blue and red lights on top of nearly every car on the road. He was a bundle of nerves, so, as he walked inside, he grabbed a bag of Cray's potato chips on one of the hooks by the registers and gripped it tightly in his fist—not too tightly, he didn't want to crush them. He'd buy it when he was done picking up whatever Bill needed, but holding it now gave him comfort.

He pulled the scrunched up wad of paper that was Bill's list out of the front pocket of his jeans and looked at it for the first time.

Jumbo-sized trash bags (Heavy duty; several boxes)
Sheet of drywall
Plaster
Air freshener (Several cans)
Lime (Several bags)
Carpet cleaner
Large fan

Jacob looked up, confused, at the row of aisle markers that hung from the ceiling, desperately wondering what half of the things on the list even were. He wasn't about to ask any of the workers for help. Drywall and plaster were home improvement items for sure, but he wondered what limes could be utilized for. He thought Bill must have made a mistake, a typo, and he wasn't about to be laughed out of the store by some hairy-faced lumberjack who'd shout to his co-workers to come and see the guy who thinks he needs a lime to mend a wall. He'd do it on his own.

He decided that his best course of action was to go through every aisle one by one and scan the shelves for the items on his list. Aisle number one was as good a start as any, and he wheeled his squeaking shopping cart to the far-left of the store and began his shopping experience.

He found himself on the paint aisle. His first inclination was to abandon it to its own devices, but there was an off-chance that the things on his list could be there. He had no way of knowing, so he went slowly down both sides of the aisle—first the left and then, turning around at the end, the right.

With a squeak, Jacob brought the cart to a sudden halt. He gripped the handles tightly, and tried to steady his rapid breathing. Standing directly in the middle of the right side of the aisle was a uniformed police officer. He was picking up different cans of paint, examining them in his hand, and then placing them back on the shelf. It was the perfect cover, and Jacob knew that the man was using his peripherals to scan his surroundings, a list of wanted criminals running like a news ticker in his brain.

Quickly and quietly as he could manage, Jacob backed the cart down towards the end of the aisle and attempted to round the corner, abandoning it as a viable location for the goods he sought. He was almost there. The loose front wheels of the cart were beginning to wobbly begin their arc into the next aisle when the officer looked up from his paint can and said, "Excuse me, sir!"

Jacob stopped in his tracks, his shoulders sinking with dread. "Yes, officer," he said as politely as he could, "can I help you?"

The officer walked towards him, his face blank. Did he have his hand on his gun? There was no way he had his hand on his gun, but, yes, his hand was clutched onto something down on his belt and Jacob thought it looked an awful lot like a pistol holster. Was this it? Had they found out already? How was that even possible? Did Mark get a call out while his throat was slit? He must have. It was the only way. He had managed to dial 911 while he was lying on the linoleum floor and bleeding out. The authorities had traced the call to Jacob's house and, now, he was getting arrested, charged with murder, and put in the electric chair. It was all happening. His life was over.

"I need to ask you a question," the officer said, coming to a stop a few feet from Jacob.

"Yes?" Jacob replied.

Was he going for his gun? Yes, he was going for his gun, reaching behind him to that leather holster. Jacob's muscles tightened, preparing his legs to break out into a full sprint.

"I need to know which one of these will look better," the officer said, producing two strips of paper, color samples, from the leather pouch next to his pistol holster. He held them up in front of Jacob's face. "I'm trying to surprise my wife. The baseboards are this greenish color, and I'm trying to decide which of these two will go with it. This one, or—wait a minute." He put the sample he held in his right hand, a reddish-yellow color, back into the pouch and withdrew a new one of yellowish-red. "This one," he said, holding it next to the sample in his left hand. "Usually she decides these things, but she takes months. I'm trying to get it done in time for her birthday."

Jacob stared, unseeing, at the colors that waved about his face. His mind was just beginning to come down from its mania, and his vision was blurred. Slowly, it came into focus. "Um, I like that one," he said at last, tapping the yellowish-red sample.

"You sure?" said the officer. "I think I like the other one better." He held both the reddish-yellow and the yellowish-red up to his eyes. "Yeah, I think I'm going with the other one. Thanks, though!" He smiled, and placed the rejected yellowish-red sample card in the place nearest him. It held blueish-purple cards.

Jacob breathed deeply as the sound of his heart's pounding slowly quieted. He quickly went down the other side of aisle one, not surprised upon finding none of the things on his list and declaring aisle one a lost cause altogether. He went down both sides of two, three, and four, doing the same. At five, he found drywall, and placed a large sheet of the stuff over top of the cart. Plaster was on the endcap, and he had to maneuver the drywall out of the way to put a tub in. On six he found jumbo-sized trash bags, air freshener, and carpet cleaner, and he stockpiled all three in his cart. Seven held nothing for him, but, on eight, he found a large, free-standing fan. It boasted three speeds, and looked more than adequate.

Now, only limes remained—if they were limes. In the middle of aisle eight, Jacob stared at the list, wondering what other word Bill could have meant to write when he wrote lime. Or, maybe, he did mean he wanted bags of limes. Maybe they were unrelated to the construction project at hand. Maybe Bill just liked limes. Jacob tried to remember if fruit flies looked different from regular house-flies, and attempted to place Bill in one camp or the other. He couldn't remember, though. Knowing that hardware stores didn't have produce depart-ments, Jacob decided that he'd stop by the grocery store on his way home to pick up the last item on his list.

Having made up his mind, he wheeled the cart to the front of the store, to the row of registers. One of the cashiers, a lady with a jet-black bun, waved for him to come into her line. As he walked towards her, he saw a word, "Lime." It was posted on several bags at an endcap on aisle one. He had somehow missed it.

"Just one second!" he said to the woman, wheeling his cart back through the store.

When he arrived at the endcap, he brought out his list and checked the spelling Bill had used—just to be safe. It was spelled the same, and in bags, so Jacob figured this had to be what Bill wanted. He slid the drywall off the top of the cart, and put four large bags inside.

"Forget something?" the woman joked as he went back up to her register.

"Yeah. I missed the limes," Jacob replied.

The woman, her name was Jacey judging by her nametag, began scanning his items. Loud *deets* sounded from her machine. They annoyed him, but he had not realized that several of the things he purchased were on sale, and that put him in a very good mood indeed.

10.

As Jacob walked to his front door, laden with the spoils of the hardware store, he noticed that Mark's bright red truck was missing. He had seen it parked along the street when he had left, but there was no sign of it now. That worried him. He opened the door and the strong stench of ammonia wafted like a cloud towards him. It made his eyes water, and his throat turn dry. He thought about the time he had gone to the hospital to see his grandfather after the stroke.

"I took care of his truck," Bill called out from somewhere beyond the hall. "Bring the stuff to the bedroom. I've got him all ready."

Bill's tone was closed to questions, so Jacob didn't ask any. With shaky hands he popped open the bag of Cray's he had bought and walked cautiously to the bedroom, afraid of the blood, entrails, brains, and gore he'd undeniably see. He saw none as he walked down the hallway, but there was plenty as he walked into the bedroom.

"Take the garbage bag, put in a section, sprinkle

it with lime, put it in another garbage bag," Bill said.

Jacob stared at the orderly, even piles of human that were laid out on newspaper in the middle of the bedroom floor. It was nearly impossible to distinguish what had once been arm, leg, or torso. Everything was simply red meat, like a butcher's shop window. Somehow, that made it easier to look at.

"Do you understand?" Bill asked.

Jacob put the bags from the hardware store down on the carpet and nodded.

"The lime will break it down much faster, and the fan and the air fresheners will help with the smell."

Jacob picked up the first pile of flesh by the newspaper it sat on and slid it into a trash bag. A portion of the mess managed to slide down the front of the bag and fall in clumps on the carpet.

"That's why we have the carpet cleaner," Bill said, "but try to be more careful."

"Okay," Jacob said. He picked up the gore with a newspaper, put it in the trash bag, and then grabbed the carpet cleaner out from one of the plastic bags and laid a thick layer of foam down on the stain.

There had been, Jacob figured, at least seven separate piles, all needing to be bagged, limed, and then bagged again. Yet, when he had finished only his third bag, he found the task complete, and the wall perpendicular to the opening in the closet stacked high with trash bags of human.

"Stack them in the closet," Bill ordered.

Jacob carefully stacked the bags in the alcove he had created earlier, pushing them and molding them until they were tightly packed. As he reached for the final bag, he noticed that there was none left, and, as he turned back to the opening in the wall, he found it completely sealed. The drywall he had bought was in shreds, whatever was leftover from cutting it to size, and the tub of plaster was open with a spreader sticking inside the white goop.

"Done," Bill said. "Open up a window and get the fan going."

Jacob was dumbfounded, concerned that, apparently, vast spaces of time were totally unaccounted for in his mind. He plugged the fan into the outlet by the nightstand, and put it on its highest setting. With a whirr, it churned to life. He went to the window—the same window that Bill had flown in the morning before—and slid it open. He could feel the heat in the air.

"We need to make sure we spritz around the fan once every twenty minutes or so," Bill said. "We need the air to circulate in here, but we can't have it expelling death-smell into the outside world. What scent did you get?"

"Uh," Jacob muttered, rifling through one of the plastic bags for the air freshener. When he found it, he brought it out and read the label. "Fine Summer's Eve."

"What the hell does that even mean?" Bill laughed. "No matter. It'll work. Why not give it a spritz now?"

Jacob walked over to the fan and held the air

freshener out at arm's length, waiting for his cue from Bill. He wasn't sure what, exactly, he was waiting for. Bill's tiny body was too small to make out his details, so he waited for a particularly boisterous flutter of the fly's wings to serve as his go ahead.

He compressed the button on top of the can, and a soft mist of fragrance shout out.

"More than that," Maddy said. "Gosh, you really went for it."

"What do you want me to say?" Jacob replied as he compressed the button again and let out a much more liberal amount of the synthesized scent. "Do you want me to apologize for my bodily functions?"

"No," she said, walking into the bathroom with her makeup bag in tow. "I just want you to use the air freshener when you stink up the whole damn apartment." She turned to him as he waved his hand through the air to spread the perfumed cloud. "That's all I ask, and I don't think that's too much."

Her lips were parted as she put on her eye-makeup—three delicate brush strokes on each lash. Jacob checked to make sure he had flushed the toilet and walked over to her.

"Sorry, I'm just *so* disgusting," he joked.

"You're not *so* disgusting, just a little bit," she smiled. "Hurry up. We've got to leave in ten minutes."

"Why not hit it once more?" Bill said, breaking Jacob from the memory.

"Sure, sure," Jacob replied, and compressed the

button again.

"That ought to do it. Do that every twenty minutes, and we'll be fine. We'll only have to do it for a few days—just until the initial stink wears off—and only then during the day, when people are around. In about a week, it'll be like he isn't even here."

"And, what, we just leave him in there, in the closet?"

"For the time being. When he's broken down a little bit, we can talk about a safe place to bury him, but not until then. We need to make sure we're clear before we go out lugging human remains."

"Okay," Jacob said simply.

"I'm taking a rest," said Bill, sounding exhausted. "I've done enough work today to last me a lifetime. You're on your own. You think you can handle it?"

"Of course."

"I like the confidence, but don't get too cocky. Don't let the 'tides of memory' sweep you away, Mr. Kingsley. Keep your head about you."

Jacob was going to ask Bill what he meant, but he suddenly wasn't around to ask anymore. That was no matter; he needed a rest as well.

Jacob washed his hands in the bathroom and finished off the half-eaten bag of Cray's he had left on the bed. He walked into the kitchen and grabbed a beer from the fridge before stomping into the living room and plopping down onto the sofa, which squeaked loudly as it received his weight.

The stench of ammonia from the bathroom

had mixed with that of the air freshener, making a scent that was awful, but not intolerable. The house seemed oddly quiet. Preemptively, Jacob switched on the GameBox and let the light and sounds of the television wash over him.

Call of Violence flashed across his eyes with an explosion and a tank running through a four foot wall, crushing cowering insurgents under its treads. Jacob's tongue slung over to the side of his mouth, and he hit the "Start" button.

He, the floating gun-sights on the bottom right corner of the screen, was running through a war-torn village. Shells were bursting overhead, and his commanding officer was standing by a dilapidated home and shouting something at him. Jacob stopped his sprint, and walked over to him.

"We've got a bunch of the bastards holed up inside," the officer said. Jacob thought he remembered his name—Briggs, or something. "We need to take them out if we're going to hold this block."

Jacob slid up against the doorway, and waited for the bright blue "A" button to appear. When it did, he turned to the door and kicked it in with all his might. The men inside were shouting in their foreign language as gunfire and smoke filled the room. One of them popped up from behind an overturned table, and Jacob put him down with three short bursts of his rifle.

"Take the left, Jacob," Officer Briggs said. "We'll take the right."

Jacob turned down the left hallway, and was greeted by two men that jumped out from adjacent doors. He took the knife in his hand and slashed both of the Mark Benjamins across their familiar throats, gasping with horror, surprise, and then recognition as he watched them fall wide-eyed to the ground.

"You had to know…you had to," the Mark Benjamins said in unison as blood spurted from their necks.

"Great job, solider," Officer Briggs said, walking over to Jacob and placing a hand on his shoulder. Only it wasn't a hand. It was a leg—a hairy black fly leg. Jacob turned and saw that Officer Briggs' face was that of an insect's, and its odd tongue was moving and clacking as the human-like, but not quite human voice said, "Great job, Jacob. Great job."

His vision abruptly rotated upward, and a thin layer of red fell downwards from the top of the screen. The score of the match was displayed, and some other player called him a fag through a cheap headset, making the words almost entirely static. Jacob let the controller fall from his hands, and it landed with a thud on the carpet. He rose from the couch and turned off both the GameBox and the television. As their glow slowly died, the room was bathed in darkness. He took a deep breath and scratched the stubble on his chin. Somehow it had gotten late, and he hadn't even had dinner yet.

11.

Robert scooped a large spoonful of fair-trade, whole-bean coffee into the top of his coffee grinder and closed the lid. He hit the start button and the machine erupted in a grinding chorus. When it had finished, he brought the grounds up to his nose and took a large whiff. He could smell the social justice, and he smiled.

He put the contents of the cup into the top of the percolator and filled it with water before hitting its start button. Soon the smell of fresh, guilt-free coffee filled his kitchen. He poured it into his travel mug and grabbed the gluten-free bagel that had popped up out of the toaster. He opened his fridge for the butter, and found that his eyes had locked with the label of a jar of strawberry jam. He still hadn't unlocked the universe's puzzle from yesterday morning. He knew he would. He just needed to be open and receptive, so he decided to spread his bagel with the strawberry jam instead of butter. It was obvious that's what fate wanted.

As his Takahashi Krius drove through the

streets of Brandon, he sipped on his coffee and tried to think of what his Sunday would hold. It was difficult to tell. It could be anything, and that's why he liked the force. A few minutes later and he was pulling into the parking lot of the police station, making sure to park in a spot next to a streetlight. He wanted his car fully visible when it got dark. A vagrant would have to be pretty daring to try something at a police station, but he wouldn't put it past them. That's one thing he had learned over the years.

As he walked up to the door of the station, he marveled at how empty the parking lot was. No one wanted to work Sundays, and Robert had only recently volunteered for the honor. He had thought he would hate it, but he actually liked having most of the office to himself. It gave him room to do his stretches and his kettlebell, and he felt like he could breathe easier without the bustle of a weekday swirling about him.

He walked inside and smiled politely at Camilla, the weekend receptionist, as he passed through into the offices. They were still dark save for the glow of a single computer that Sergeant Frank Butler sat behind.

"Are you turning into a bat, Frank?" Robert said, flipping on the light switch.

"Huh?" Frank muttered, his eyes still fixed on the luminescent screen.

"You're just sitting in here with the lights off."

"Yeah," Frank said absently. He wheeled out from the desk and produced two color samples from one of the drawers. "Hey, I'm doing something for Nancy—trying to repaint the living room for her birthday—and I can't for the ever-loving life of me decide on what color to use. Can I get your opinion?"

"Yeah, sure," Robert said, walking over to his desk. Staring at him was a note written in pen.

Woman assaulted at her convenience store on Grissom. Says it was a big guy in a factory uniform. Check it out.

A phone number and address were attached on a second sheet. Robert knew the message was from Chief Merriweather. Evidently this was his work for the day. He had hoped for something more exciting, but, then again, those always went to the younger detectives. Despite his years on the force, he simply wasn't popular. His methods were deemed too eccentric by nicer people, and absolute insanity by the more free-speaking folk. Robert didn't understand the stigma. He always got results.

"So I'm thinking this greenish-blue," Frank said, holding the cards up to Robert's face. "What do you think?"

"Yeah, that's good," Robert answered.

"Did you even look at them?"

Robert wheeled his chair out from his desk and placed the glasses that hung from a string around his neck onto the slender bridge of his nose. He squinted at the samples, trying to remember what color the baseboards were in the Butler living room. He had been over for dinner a few times. Frank was one of the nice ones.

"I'm actually thinking that reddish one," Robert said after some time.

"The yellowish-red one?"

"Yeah."

Frank held the card in question up to his eyeballs and grimaced. "No, no, that's not it at all. You're way off."

"Well, it was only my opinion."

"Well, your opinion stinks!" Frank shouted, his face growing red as he stormed off, wheeling his desk chair behind him.

"Frank," Robert called after him imploringly.

His words were met with the back of Frank's head.

"Frank, c'mon!" Robert said, slightly annoyed this time.

When he arrived at his desk, Frank plopped down into the chair, scowled, and gave Robert the middle finger. "I was just trying to get your advice. You didn't have to be such a jerk."

Robert shook his head and fired up his computer with a slight, nervous grin. He wondered if Frank had taken his medication, but knew it was none of his business. The welcome screen had just come up, and he had only just taken the electronic timer out from his desk drawer, when the intercom sounded with a crackle.

"Detective," Camilla's voice sounded.

He pushed the tiny gray button and leaned down close to the speaker. "Yeah, I'm here."

"I'm buzzing a woman in to talk to you. Says her boyfriend's been missing."

This was perfect. The only thing worse than tracking down old lady beaters was listening to sobbing girlfriends lament over how they can't find their deadbeat boyfriends. Inevitably the boyfriends turn up—reeking of booze and cigarettes—but they turn up. Missing person cases were almost always a waste of time.

"Is she there with you?" he asked, fully intending to dismiss her if she wasn't within earshot of the intercom.

"Yeah, she's right here."

Shit. "Alright, send her in," he said, grabbing a pencil and pad of paper from his desk. It was important that he looked busy to her, but, in reality, he had watched several videos on the internet about how to draw realistic anime characters, and he planned to get a little practice in.

The door to the offices opened and in she walked. Her brown hair was pulled back in a ponytail, which fell down against her bare shoulders and twisted along the yellow tank-top she wore. Thin streaks, doubtlessly tear stains, ran through the small amount of foundation on her face, and her lips were coated lightly with pink lipstick. She looked like she was about to burst into tears anew, and Robert braced himself for a long, tiresome discussion.

"Morning, ma'am," he said in the most official tone he could muster. "How can I help?"

"Hey," she sighed, sitting down at the chair in front of his desk. Her eyes passed from window to window, from desk to desk, from wall to wall, but they never met his gaze. Her shoulders rose and fell.

"Need a place to start?" Robert said. "How about your name, please."

"Oh, yeah, sorry. Emily Grainger."

Robert nodded, gripped his pencil tightly, and began the first stroke for the girl's left eye. The eyes were always the most important part. If you got a good anime eye down, you could easily incorporate the rest. After a few seconds, and a few failed attempts, he looked up.

"And what's the matter, now?"

"My boyfriend didn't come home last night. I haven't seen or heard from him since yesterday morning."

"I see," Robert said, trying desperately to get that iris right. "And what is his name?"

"Mark Benjamin."

"Uh huh," Robert said. He was preoccupied. He had just drawn the perfect eye—with just the right amount of twinkle and arc. Now he only needed to do the other…

"Don't you need to know where he was last?" the woman asked.

"Yes, that will certainly help."

"I sent him over to a co-worker of ours' house. His name's Jacob Kingsley."

"Uh huh."

"See, he wanted to ask me out—Jacob that is— and I told him yes 'cause I really didn't want to hurt his feelings. I decided later that I made a mistake by getting his hopes up and I sent Mark over to clear things up. I was too scared. I guess I'm not good with confrontation."

"Mmhmm."

"And that was the last I heard from him. I think you need to check Jacob's house."

"Shit," Robert muttered. He had botched it—totally and irrevocably. The left eye was perfect, but the right looked like a disfigured lima bean with a spot of mold in the middle where the pupil should be. He couldn't understand the discrepancy.

"Pardon me?" Emily said, confused.

"No, no, it's not you," Robert stuttered, looking up at the girl. "It's just—"

He stopped. His eyes began to water, and his pulse quickened to what must have been 130, or even 160. In the girl's hair, pinning back a particularly rebellious bit of bangs that threatened to fall into her eyes, was a hair clip—a hair clip in the shape of a strawberry. It was pink, and bore the fruit prominently on its top side. This was no coincidence. This was fate, the universe, giving him a key.

"I'm sorry—terribly sorry—miss," Robert said, ripping his failed drawing from the pad of paper and starting a new, clean sheet. He renewed the grip on his pencil, his eyes fixed on the strawberry. "Please, tell me everything—in detail."

12.

There was just something about the way the yolk leaked out of his morning eggs that Sunday that made Jacob queasy. He watched it slowly slink towards the side of his plate, drenching his sausages in the yellowy liquid. His appetite was gone, and that was certainly nothing to take lightly. He couldn't remember a time when his appetite was gone.

"Something not to your liking?" Bill asked, taking his sustenance from a spot of grease on Jacob's plate.

"No, everything's great. Thank you."

"You sure you're alright?"

"Yeah, I think so."

Bill flew up to Jacob's shoulder and cleaned his legs with his tiny mouthpiece. "Listen. You've been through a lot," he said. "Breakups aren't easy. They take a lot out of person. You need some time to rest and recuperate."

He paused, and Jacob could hear the soft chirping of a bird—probably in the large Guajillo tree outside.

"Why don't you go outside for a while?" Bill said. "It's a lovely day. Get out of this stuffy old house and experience it. Go out to the mall or something. It'll be good for you."

"What would I do at the mall?"

"Anything. Get a pretzel."

Jacob pushed his plate into the middle of the table and stood up. It was true. The air inside of the house was stuffy, constricting. It made it hard to breathe. Maybe it would do him some good to get out. It certainly couldn't hurt.

"Okay," Jacob said simply, and grabbed his keys from the kitchen counter.

He generously spritzed the bedroom, put on his shoes, and opened the front door. Bill buzzed after him, landing on his shoulder. "I hope you don't mind me coming along," Bill said.

Jacob didn't answer.

He climbed into his truck, started it up, and backed out of the driveway. There was no destination in his mind. He was just driving. He rolled down the windows and let the dry, dusty air filter into the cabin. He didn't mind it so much.

Somehow, his drive took him onto Grissom Street, but he didn't look at Javelina Good Time as he passed it. He kept his gaze straight forward— upon the open road. The buildings slowly faded, leaving in their wake only dust, dirt, and desert. Occasionally a cactus or brittlebush would rise up, but these were few and far between. All was flat and barren.

The buzzing of Bill had gone, and Jacob had

barely noticed its passing.

The roads in Arizona weren't like the ones back east. Those twisted and turned, dipping and rising with the hills and valleys. Here, everything was flat— monotonous. Jacob remembered when he had first come upon the flatness, driving through the night, away from everything he had ever known, but, most of all, away from Maddy. He had driven because there was nothing for him in Connecticut, and he couldn't stand the idea that there existed a Maddy who was happy, healthy, whole, and perfectly content—maybe even more content—without him.

His foot came off of the accelerator and depressed the brake pedal. Slowly, the truck squealed to a stop. It sat in the middle of the lane, and Jacob climbed out. Wind whipped gently across the plains, and filled him with a queer melancholy both cathartic and terrible. He watched the clouds of dust drift, and he imagined himself drifting as well—light as a feather, going wherever the wind took him. Maybe that was his motivation for driving west those months ago. He was trying to be weightless.

He stood silent for a long while, watching the swirling wind and listening to the chirps of the birds. Then the whine of the wind was broken by the gurgling of Jacob's stomach. He was hungry now. He climbed back into his truck and turned it back the way he had come. He knew there was a Burger Duke on the corner of Grissom and Jay, and he yearned for it.

Sometime during the course of the drive back

into town, he noticed that Bill was trying desperately to cling to his shirt as the wind whipped violently through the truck's cabin. He was attached only by one of his small, slender legs, and even that was shaking, threating to relinquish its grip. Jacob rolled the windows up, cutting off the wind and allowing Bill to take his comfortable place on his shoulder. The fly buzzed cheerily.

13.

Robert gently closed the door of his Takahashi
Krius, and observed his surroundings with his
hands placed firmly on his hips. He thought they
felt a little doughy, and decided he would throw in
an extra fifteen crunches that evening in an effort to
rectify the problem. The Gaujillo tree outside the
house was rustling in the wind, and Robert pulled
out the handkerchief he kept in his pocket. He
wrapped it around his mouth and nose to protect
from the dust, looking very much like a bandit in an
old western film. Locking his car, he walked up the
driveway of the home and rang the doorbell.

The front porch was entirely non-descript—no
signs of personality at all. There wasn't even a rug
by the door. Robert looked down at his shoes, dismayed at the thin white layer of concrete dust that
was caking them. He bent down and brushed them
off, but now the dust was on his hands. He be-
grudgingly wiped them off on his slacks. He waited
for a few seconds, and then opened the screen door
and knocked.

As he did, a truck pulled into the driveway. Robert turned around and put his hands back on his hips, getting into his "detective" role using some of the Buddhist breathing exercises he had discovered on masterjim.com. A large, stocky man climbed out of the truck and Robert walked cautiously, but—he hoped—confidently towards him.

"Good afternoon, sir," he said, slipping the bandanna from his mouth.

The stocky man wiped a bit of hamburger bun from his plain white t-shirt, and looked up dumbly. "Good afternoon," he replied plainly.

"Are you Jacob Kingsley?"

Jacob's heart started up with its frantic beating again. Was this guy a cop? This was worse than the hardware store, but he knew, if he kept his cool, it would end just as innocuously. "Yeah. That's me," he said.

"I'm Detective Robert Killian with the Brandon Police. Do you mind if I ask you a few questions?"

"Keep it cool," Bill said, perched on the tip of Jacob's ear.

"Sure. What about?" Jacob asked.

Robert stood in his place and watched Jacob for a few, brief seconds. He was trying to gauge the man's character, and, usually, he was pretty good at it. There were extremely subtle, unconscious muscle movements in the face that could reveal whether someone was lying. However, none seemed to show on Mr. Kingsley. The girlfriend had given him a picture of Mark Benjamin, and Robert walked over to Jacob and took it out of his pocket.

"Have you seen this guy?" he asked, handing the photo to Jacob.

Jacob took it in his hand and squinted at it, trying to determine what to say.

"It won't do to lie," Bill said. "They'll know that you worked with him. Keep it surface level."

Confused, Robert asked, "Can you see the photograph, sir?"

"Yeah, yeah, I can see it," Jacob replied. "I work with this guy. His name is Mark, I think."

"Mark Benjamin," Robert said.

"Yeah. That's it," Jacob said, handing the photo back to him, happy to rid that smiling face from his hand.

"He's been missing since yesterday morning," Robert said, tucking the photograph into his pocket. "You haven't seen him, have you?"

"Not since Friday. He works the morning shift. I usually see him at the time clock when I come in."

"So, you haven't seen him since Friday, then?"

This was almost over. "No. Not since Friday," Jacob said.

Robert nodded to himself, and Jacob couldn't tell if it was nervousness or confidence that had prompted the action. "Well, my source tells me that you were the last person to see him alive," Robert said, a smirk forming on his lips.

"W-what do you mean? What are you saying?" Jacob said, his mouth moving faster than his mind. He was still trying to comprehend the implications of the detective's words. Was he a suspect?

"Keep it together, Jacob," Bill said.

Maybe I'm coming on too strong, Robert thought. There was no reason to push the guy too hard. It had only been a day. Mark Benjamin could still show up, completely unscathed. It had happened before, and, in fact, it was the norm. But there was that strawberry hair clip and its universal significance and he had been brought to the home of Jacob Kingsley for a reason.

"I'm not saying anything," he said. "The man's missing, and I'm told you were the last person to speak with him. I'm following my leads. So, would you like to retract your previous statement?"

"Would I what?" Jacob said, his mind still reeling.

"Calm the fuck down," said Bill.

"Did you or did you not see Mark Benjamin yesterday morning?"

"It's obvious that Emily is his so-called 'source.' She probably told him that she sent Mark to cancel her date for her—like a cowardly bitch," Bill said. "There's no use denying you've seen him. We need to send him off course. Make something up."

"Yeah, but what?" Jacob said.

"Yeah, you did see him?" Robert asked.

"I don't know," said Bill. "Anything—anything to get him off of us."

"Yeah," Jacob said, trying desperately to think of something and immensely worried that he was coming off as suspicious. "I did see him. I'm sorry, I forgot. It was only briefly in the morning."

"Tell me about it," Robert said, getting out his pad and paper and flipping past dozens of drawings of failed anime eyes.

"Huh?"

"Tell me what happened."

"He came over and we talked."

"About what?"

"I don't really recall."

"So, it was just a social visit?"

"Yeah."

"My source told me that Mark was sent over to cancel a date you had that night."

"No, no, that's not what happened at all," Jacob said. He could feel the blood at the back of his neck again. "You're wrong."

"So, you didn't talk about the cancelled date at all?"

"No. We didn't. Nothing was cancelled."

"You went on the date, then?"

"Yes. It was lovely. We lingered on her porch, and we kissed before she left."

Robert stared at him, trying to find the cues that he was lying. There was nothing. Jacob returned the stare with a stone-cold look of his own. "And what was the name of the girl?" Robert asked.

"Emily Grainger," Jacob replied, his shoulders rising and falling rapidly. The name hurt to say.

"Okay, so, did Mark say where he was going after he left that morning?"

"Now's your chance," said Bill.

"Um, yeah, yeah, he said he was going to go visit his mother."

"His mother?"

"Yes."

"Do you know his mother?"

"No, I've never met her."

"Any idea where she lives?"

"Not one."

Robert closed his notepad and tucked it back into his pocket. "Okay. Thank you, Jacob. You've been very helpful."

"Okay," Jacob said. He watched as the detective got into his car, backed out of the driveway, and drove away.

"He'll be back," Bill said when he was gone.

"I know," Jacob replied.

"Any ideas?"

Jacob squinted into the noonish sun and said, "We run."

14.

Every ounce of food in the home was haphazardly packed into leftover plastic grocery bags. They sat on the bed while Jacob scrabbled madly about, packing anything he thought he might ever need. The GameBox came next, and he wrapped it with plastic bags and duct tape and placed it, too, on the pile of necessities he had formed upon the old, yellowed comforter.

"When they see we're gone, they're going to come looking for us," Bill said, flying this way and that, reflecting the mania that Jacob openly expressed.

"I know that. I know that!" Jacob said, flinging clothes onto the pile as well. "We're dropping off the radar."

"Easier said than done," Bill said.

"Shut up."

As he threw the last coat onto the pile, Jacob realized that the day had slipped away from him. He was standing in darkness, having forgotten in his franticness to even flip on the light switch. He checked his alarm clock. It was eight o'clock, and he was incredibly tired. He sat down on the edge of the bed and breathed deeply.

"We're going to have to take him with us," Bill said, pointing one hairy leg towards the closet. "I'm sure they'll have no problem getting a search warrant, and they'll tear this place apart when they find we skipped town."

"Okay," Jacob said.

He was exhausted, and needed a drink. However, his fatigue got the better of him and he collapsed, fully-dressed and half-packed, on the pile of his belongings.

He woke. It being a Monday, his alarm clock was still set for the usual time. He angrily pounded the snooze button and rolled over onto his side, fully intending to give himself a few more hours' rest. Then the realization hit him. Today was the day of flight. He shot up from bed and tried desperately to make the pile of clothes, food, and belongings somewhat organized. He didn't know how long it took to get a warrant, but he wanted to be far away by the time they had one.

He didn't own a proper suitcase, but he figured he could tie everything up hobo-style in his comforter. He was just beginning to form the logistics of such an action when a timid knock sounded on his door. He froze in his place. The path was set before him, now, there was no turning back. If they were coming for him, he would have to fight his way out. He was running.

The knock sounded again. He contemplated escaping through the window, but he had no idea how many patrol cars they had out front. He didn't want to get shot as soon as he poked his head out.

"Answer the damn door," Bill said, landing on the pile on the bed. "I doubt a SWAT team coming to apprehend you would politely knock."

There was sense in that, and Jacob walked cautiously to the door. As he passed by the kitchen, he grabbed a knife from the block, but, as he looked at it in his hand, he began to feel sick. He opted for an empty beer bottle by the couch instead.

He opened the front door and Emily was standing there. She was like a dream. She wasn't dressed in her usual work-attire, but wore a tight-fitting t-shirt and jeans. Her hair was devoid of her signature pony tail and fell loosely, beautifully about her shoulders. Even her lipstick was pinker than usual, glistening upon her full lips. The lips moved, and a wavering voice filtered out.

"Can I come in?" it said.

Jacob was stunned into silence, staring at the vision of beauty that had only ever graced his front porch in his most private fantasies.

"Pick your jaw off the floor and let her in!" Bill said in Jacob's ear before landing on the solitary pocket of his white t-shirt.

"Would you like to come in?" Jacob asked her at last.

She didn't look at him, and kept her head down as she passed through the doorway. Jacob closed the door behind her, and stood awkwardly in the space between the dining room card table and the living room pile of empty beer bottles. He felt em-barrassed.

"Can I get you anything?" he said, breaking the silence and walking into the kitchen, leaving Emily standing by the front door. He opened the fridge and found it warm and empty. He forgot that he was planning to flee—leaving him with nothing to offer her. Gritting his teeth, he mentally kicked himself for being so stupid. Why couldn't he have waited until the afternoon to make his desperate flight? Then, he would have had something to offer the woman he loved when she showed up inexpli-cably on his front door. This was his one chance, and he was ruining it. Maybe he could find some-thing he had forgotten to pack. Maybe in the cup-boards?

"That's okay. I don't need anything," Emily said plainly. The emotion in her voice had dried up somewhat, leaving a strange inflection that was fa-miliar to Jacob, though he couldn't place it.

"Not even a coffee?" Jacob asked, knowing full-well that there was no coffee to give. She didn't have to know that, though. The fact that he offered was all that mattered. She'd say no anyhow.

"Okay, I'll take some coffee," she said.

"Fuck," escaped his lips, and he quickly turned around towards the front door to see if she had heard him. If she had, she'd showed no sign of it.

There were still a few coffee mugs left in the cabinet—the chipped ones that he didn't want to take with him—and he filled two of them up with water and brought them out by the door. It was better than nothing.

"Well, the coffee seems to be misplaced, but we do have good, old fashioned city wat—what's wrong?"

Emily was sitting with her back against the door, trying her best to suck up the tears that flowed from her red eyes and slid down her cheeks. "Have you seen Mark?"

"Mark?" Jacob asked. The word served as a placeholder until he could think of something else to say.

"Yes. I sent him over here. Did he talk to you?"

"No, I haven't seen him since Friday at work."

"Jesus," she whimpered, and the tears came anew.

Jacob crouched down in front of her, bending his legs down beneath his large body. Now was his chance. He knew he could bring her around to his side if he showed her sympathy—gave her a shoulder to cry on. She would accept his kindness, incredibly touched, and they'd be between the covers of his bed by the afternoon. Of course, he'd have to move the pile of belongings first. He was sure he could think of something to explain that, but first…

"Did something happen, Emily?" he asked in the kindest sounding tone he could muster.

"He was supposed to go and talk to you," she whimpered. "Why didn't he talk to you?"

Jacob gently placed his hand on her heaving shoulder. "I don't know. I don't, but I forgive you for standing me up the other night. It's obvious that you're going through a lot."

That was it. He was saying all the right things. The only trouble was that Emily didn't seem to be responding. They were supposed to share an appreciative glance that would slowly morph into a smile, the first spark of romance, but she kept looking at the floor. Jacob gently curled his forefinger and placed it under her chin, lifting her head up towards his. Her eyes glistened, and Jacob wanted badly to kiss her. He waited for the smile. That would be his signal, the thing telling him that she would be his, the opening of the door. Yet her face was blank, and he didn't understand.

He stared at her—her eyes glistening, her face flushed, her cheeks rosy with only a touch of blush, her pink lipstick looking pinker than ever. And he kissed her.

His lips received her warmth and sent an electric shock that resonated within every muscle. A shockwave passed through his entire body, and he felt euphoria seep into his brain. For a split second it was as if Emily's lips moved against his, but then the second was over.

"What the fuck!" she shouted, pushing him off of her.

He fell backwards, losing his balance, and landed flat on his back. Emily got to her feet and turned towards the door. He could see her shapely backside drifting away from him forever. He propped himself up and grabbed hold of the only part of her within reach, her left ankle. She tripped and fell head-first, smashing hard into the closed front door, her body folding into a tight clump of clothes, limbs, and curves.

15.

The sand was cool beneath his feet, and it was almost orgasmic to curl his bare toes and plunge them inside it. The sun was just beginning to set on the horizon. Seagulls cried out high overhead, and Jacob craned his neck to try and see them. Despite the clarity of the skies, he couldn't make out where they were. He propped himself up on his flimsy cloth lounge chair, trying his best to find a comfortable position to ease the growing ache in his upper thighs. They felt tired, overworked, and Jacob realized that he needed another drink.

He motioned to Maddy, who stood nearby, and she produced for him a fresh Mai-Tai, smiling as she did. He smiled back. No verbal words of thanks were needed. They had transcended that, the two of them. He placed his lips around the straw and sucked in the fruity liquid. It was cool and refreshing on his palate.

He turned to his right and saw Emily's silhouette walking slowly along the shore. She looked beautiful, and he called out to her. Her brown hair, freed from her ponytail, blew gently, wafting in the breeze. But she didn't turn her head towards him.

"Emily, come here!" he shouted again, louder this time. The waves crashed louder than they had before, and he realized that they were probably too loud for Emily to hear him. He briefly glanced at Maddy, who still stood smiling at his side, and rose from the lounge chair.

His head felt light, and he wondered how many drinks he had had. Slowly, he began to walk towards Emily, finding her much farther away than she had seemed from the lounge chair, and his feet far heavier than he ever remembered them being. With each step, his chest fired with pain. It felt as if a twelve ton truck was slowly crushing him to death.

"Emily," he called, gasping, "come here."

He heard her laugh, and saw her silhouette skip further away down the shore.

"Damn it, Emily!" he shouted, feeling the words tax him considerably.

He watched in desperation as her figure shrunk smaller and smaller, slipping away from him. Then he heard her scream. His feet were lighter now, and he found the strength to break out into a sprint. He ran towards the tiny speck of her silhouette, now crumpled in a heap on the ground. Something small was darting about her, flying this way and that and prodding her as she cried out in pain and flailed her arms and legs.

"Bill, get off of her!" Jacob screamed, his teeth bearing down hard on his lower jaw.

Bill stopped, and turned towards Jacob as he

approached. The knife from the kitchen was wrapped in one of his tiny legs, and he lunged deftly towards Jacob, who only barely dodged out of the way in time. As he ducked, he glanced at the bleeding and broken body of Emily lying motionless in a heap.

"You bastard!" he shouted. "You killed her!"

Bill lunged again with the knife, but Jacob's anger fueled him. Despite being cut deep by the blade on his arm, he brought his hand colliding against the black speck of Bill's body, which sent Bill flying through the air and sent the knife falling into the sand.

For a moment, Jacob was on his guard, ready to combat the fly wherever he came from next. But he never came. He listened for the tell-tale buzz of Bill's wings, but the only sounds were the invisible sea gulls and the gentle slapping of the surf upon the shore.

Jacob breathed deeply, and bent down towards Emily. She was cut badly, lacerations covering her naked arms, legs, and thighs. He cradled her head in his hands, and began to cry. He waited for her chest to rise as life-giving oxygen filtered in through her lungs, but it never did. She was gone.

He raised her lips to his and he kissed her. He kissed her and tried not to think of her lips connecting with Mark Benjamin's. He tried not to think of the many times Mark Benjamin had held her in his arms and the many times she had smiled, feeling safe and secure, in response. He tried not to think of their naked bodies entwined between the sheets of Mark's bed. He tried, but he failed.

He looked down and noticed that his fingers had dug deep into the flesh of her neck, causing dark purple bruises. He relinquished his grip and her head plopped down onto the pillow of his bed. His belongings were strewn all around the room, most of them congregating by the closet, crushed and broken. Blood was what he saw next—bright and red, staining the sheets of his bed and spattering the carpet and walls in strange, unnatural places. He looked down and saw the purple bruises in Emily's neck, and the lacerations in her naked, arms, legs, and thighs.

Bill sat on the headboard, buzzing quietly to himself.

"You bastard!" Jacob shouted. "You killed her!"

Bill flew upwards, deftly avoiding Jacob's assault, and hovered a few inches from the ceiling. "Don't pin this on me, Jacob," he said. "You can put yourself in whatever 'happy place' you want to put yourself in, but you can't blame this on me."

Jacob noticed that the bloody kitchen knife was sitting on the headboard, right where Bill had been.

"I'm a fly, Jacob! How could I lift that thing! I know it's easier to think that a talking fly is the personification of all your problems. It's harder to say that all your problems are precisely that—*yours.*"

Jacob looked down and saw that, now, the knife was in his hand. Disgusted, he flung it on the ground and looked up vehemently at Bill.

"I didn't put it there, Jacob. It's been there all

along. You put it on the headboard—trying to pin it on me in your little mind-vacation while you were sipping on Mai-Tais. It's the same thing you did with her boyfriend. I'm actually impressed. You took it a step further this time; invented an entirely new sensory experience."

"What are you talking about?" Jacob said. The rage had left him. Now only the sickening feeling of regret and repulsion remained—a one-two punch he was sure he'd feel for the rest of his life.

"You know what I'm talking about. No more pretending. I'm a fly. I can't kill people. I can't make you breakfast, and I can't clean your messes up for you anymore."

The blood was burning at the back of Jacob's neck, and a *deet* as loud as the cracking of the earth erupted from somewhere very close. The knife was in Bill's wiry, hairy leg, and Jacob would listen to his lies no more. It was Bill who had gotten him into all of this. He had told him to get flowers for Emily, he had doubtlessly killed Mark Benjamin too. Jacob had seen how he could bend space and time—move objects. Bill had put the knife in his hand then, and he had put the knife in his hand now. Jacob was nothing but a patsy for a hateful, murdering insect. But Bill wasn't an insect. He was something else entirely.

"Fine. Believe what you want," Bill said. "It's all you've ever done anyhow."

Jacob raged, swatting Bill out of the air and sending him careening downwards. His black body landed, dazed, on the side of Jacob's white t-shirt, and Jacob brought his open palm down hard on top of him, silencing the frantic buzzing of his wings.

16.

Robert carefully peeled the tinfoil lid off his yogurt. He plucked a napkin from the pile in the passenger's seat and wrapped the lid inside, tucking the bundle into the left pocket of his tracksuit pants. He always wore his black tracksuit on stakeout. It was comfortable, allowed him to move freely, and the black color was intimidating. He took out a plastic spoon from the zip-bag under the napkins and dunked it inside the pink, gloppy mixture. He scooped and brought the spoonful of yogurt to his expectant lips—strawberry flavored.

He wasn't usually a consumer of flavored yogurt. He found it much too high in sugar, and it was nearly impossible to trust the multitudes of health-claims printed on the food's packaging. But it was just about the only moderately healthy thing in the convenience store down the road, and he definitely needed something to munch on to pass the time. The fact that strawberry was the only flavor they carried had cemented his decision.

He picked up the binoculars around his neck,

put them up to his eyes, and peered through his windshield at the Kingsley house for about the billionth time that day. The paperwork was in. The warrant would be delivered, but in due time. Robert hated "duc time" because it always took far more time than was due. He didn't want the trail to get cold and, with Mr. Kingsley being his only lead, he had decided to scope him out to see if there was probable cause for a search. "Probable cause" was the buzzword these days, and it could apply to just about anything. He knew the guy was lying, and he really wished that a thick haze of marijuana smoke would waft out from the rear window of the house, but that would be too perfect. He'd have to wait for something else. The only thing that *might* be something was that there was a car in the driveway that Robert hadn't seen the day before. A beaten up, faded coupe. If he was in a patrol car he would have just run the tag numbers, but he was trying to keep inconspicuous, and he couldn't call the numbers into the station because he didn't have a search warrant or that desired "probable cause." So, for now, he'd have to wait.

In the meantime, he'd work on his Kegels. It was the only real exercise he could do in the cramped space of his Krius, and, although historically considered a woman's exercise, he had recently read an article saying they could prevent incontinent bladders in men. His bladder was fine now, but that didn't mean it was always going to be. It was better to be safe than sorry.

He pulled the electronic timer out from the

glove box and set it for fifteen minutes. That would give him enough time to get a good workout in. When the fifteen minutes passed, he'd set it for another fifteen, take a long swig of mineral water from the bottle in the passenger's seat, and wait for it to go off. Then he'd set it for another fifteen and do some more Kegels. It was a good plan, and he wondered why he had spent the last three hours not thinking of it.

After his fifteen minute break, as he was entering into his second set, he noticed movement. The door to the house opened and Mr. Kingsley walked outside. He looked nervous, but there wasn't any one action that told Robert that. It was just in Mr. Kingsley's walk, in the way he looked at the car in the driveway, and in the way he slowly, maybe even restrainedly, walked back inside.

Robert cleared the timer and put it back in the glove box as he reached for his binoculars. Through the lenses, he could see movement behind the small, oval window in Mr. Kingsley's front door. It was a jerking movement, like someone carrying something very heavy. He reached for his pad and tried his best to write down what he saw, still keeping his gaze fixed through the binoculars. He could discern the slanted lines and scribbles later. All that mattered was that they were there to be discerned—documented.

Minutes passed and Mr. Kingsley emerged from the doorway carrying a bright red canister of gasoline. He wobbled as he walked over to the mystery car in the driveway, and set the canister down on the ground. He fumbled in his pocket and produced a set of keys. A bit of pink shone in the sunlight, and Robert honed in on it with the binoculars. It was a small, pink bear keychain. Mr. Kingsley put the key in the lock and opened the car door, placing the can of gasoline in the back seat. He then walked back up the driveway to lock the front door, since he had neglected to before, bore down with the weight of the gasoline.

Robert put down the binoculars and buckled his seatbelt. Maybe getting into a strange vehicle with a can of gasoline wasn't *exactly* "probable cause," but it was close enough. Besides, fate had decided that Mr. Jacob Kingsley was the object of his attention, and he would listen to fate for as long as she was speaking to him. His discarded yogurt container sat on the passenger's seat, half-way wrapped in a napkin so as to avoid spillage. He looked at its pink letters and smiled.

The beaten-down coupe began its descent down the driveway, its one working brake light shining brightly, and then sped off down the neighborhood road. Robert put his Krius into gear, and followed behind at a distance. His eyes passed from the road to the notepad propped between the steering wheel and his right hand, and he scribbled furiously with the pen in his left so as not to miss a thing.

17.

He had left Emily rotting on the bed, too frightened to do what he knew must be done. He knew he'd have to clean up Bill's mess, and probably in the same way Bill had disposed of Mark Benjamin. The fly deserved credit. He knew how to hide a body. But, for now, Jacob wouldn't think about that. Cutting Emily's beautiful figure up into manageable sizes was an unpleasantness for another time. Right now, he had to get rid of a larger body of evidence.

He drove in the same direction he had the day before—through town, past the convenience store on Grissom, and straight onto the desert flats. The windows of Emily's coupe remained steadfastly shut however, and Jacob kept the wind and the outside far away from the air-conditioned environment of the car's interior. He turned the fan on the instrument panel up all the way though, and let it blow freely along his scalp.

He wished it was dark, but knew that the sun wouldn't set for several more hours. He could make do. No one ever drove on the lonely two-lane roads from Brandon, and he wouldn't be seen.

He drove for as long as he could stand and then made a sharp right and flew off the asphalt pavement, careening madly through the flats, trying his best to avoid the deeper holes and obstacles that might bring the low-riding coupe to a halt. He zoomed past cacti that seemed as tall as skyscrapers, and weaved in and out of rows of bushes and shrubs while tiny brown creatures darted in panic. More than once he thought he felt their small bodies being obliterated underneath the front tires.

He drove until he could no longer see the road in his rearview mirror and brought the car to a slow stop. He put it in park and climbed out, taking the can of gasoline with him. He'd have to make quick work of the car. He didn't have a whole lot of time. When he was done he could walk the few miles back to the road and call a taxi. He was sure they'd charge him a fortune, and he'd probably end up paying more if the driver started asking questions, but it was the only option he had. The car had to go. There was no getting around it.

He poured the gasoline over the seats and upholstery in the car's interior, and casually switched to dousing the dashboard, paying extra attention on the VIN plate. That needed to be decimated most of all—he had seen detective shows before. There was still about a quarter of the can left when he was finished, and he poured this over the hood and top of the car until only scattered, lonely droplets trickled out.

He tossed the can aside and reached into his

pocket. Everything was ready now. He brought out the lighter and took off his left shoe. He let it fall in the sand and removed his sock. He brought it up to the lighter's flame, and it caught easily, despite being damp with sweat. He mentally checked that everything truly was ready. The gasoline can was certainly empty; its contents were drenching the car. He had his lighter, his sock. Yes, everything was ready. He tossed the burning bit of fabric through the air towards the gasoline-soaked car, and heard his cellphone ring *from inside*.

He desperately clutched at his right pocket and found it horrifyingly empty, but it was too late. The car erupted in a ball of flame with an enormous boom, sending him flying off his feet through the air. He collided against something hard and unyielding with a loud clang, landing painfully several feet away. He picked himself up off the ground, shaking his stupefaction but unable to shake the notion that he had seen Maddy's number on the blue-illumined screen of his phone before it was obliterated in the fiery inferno.

He turned towards the object he'd hit, feeling pain shoot down his spine. He took several steps backwards, cocking his head sideways, trying to determine what he was looking at. After a few long seconds, he realized what it was. It was the metal skeleton of a truck. It had been torched—no doubt about it. It was blackened and charred, and a gasoline can quite like the one he had just used on Emily's car sat half-melted against a cactus nearby. Despite the damage, Jacob could tell that the truck's color had been red.

His feet gave out from under him, and he fell down, exhausted. He panted heavily as he watched the flames leap skyward off Emily's burning car, destroying and concealing the evidence of Bill's heinous crime forever. Even if the police did manage to find the charred skeleton of the vehicle—either of the vehicles—there was no way they'd be able to identify it. They were ghosts now—invisible, and, most importantly, untraceable.

The flames began to die down, and Jacob stood clumsily to his feet, discovering that the smoke had done something to his lungs. He hoped it wasn't cancer. Just about anything could turn into cancer these days. He'd have to get himself checked out when he got back into town. You could never be too careful.

He turned in the direction he thought the road was and tried to figure out a way *to* get back into town. His phone was toast—nothing but melted plastic and metal. Calling a cab was entirely out of the question. The only thing clear to him was that he had to get to the road. Maybe he could thumb a ride? He really didn't have to get back into Brandon. He had a wallet full of cash. He really just needed a place to crash—civilization. Just a bed with running water and a diner nearby. That's all he needed, but, first, the road.

Turning around in a circle, he realized that the terrain was really quite similar no matter which way he looked. He thought the bushes, towering cacti, and dead animal corpses would serve as his breadcrumbs back, but he saw plenty of those, and it didn't matter if he was looking north, south, east or what-have-you. He was wholly lost.

Despite his directional impairment, he decided that his best course of action was to move. He was bound to run into something sooner or later, and something was better than vast nothingness. He knew that much. He began to walk, keeping his back to the slowly dying fire of Emily's car.

He walked for hours, stopping only to wonder what the hell he was doing. Walking seemed like a stupid idea now, and he was no closer to anything resembling civilization. It was all just sand and shrubs. The sun began to set behind the sandy plain, and Jacob's spirits went along with it.

Suddenly, up ahead in the distance, loomed two large, white eyes. They hovered and bounced in the air, gliding along the surface of the ground and coming right towards him. They were the white of Maddy's breasts bobbing up and down in rhythm, and they were the white of his dead mother's cheek pressed firmly against his own. Mostly though, they were the headlights of a police cruiser.

The lights were joined by several others, and then by whirring red and blue ones that sat atop them like a hat. The cruisers skidded to a quick halt, and a brown-haired man in a tight-fitting black tracksuit climbed out of the car closest to him. His gold badge gleamed in the dark, reflecting the light.

"Jacob Kingsley," the man said, "you're under arrest in connection with the disappearance of Mark Benjamin."

18.

Jacob was brought into a tiny room. In its center was a long metal table with a chair on one side. He was surprised how much TV had prepared him for this. He was sure that two black-suited cops would come in—one older, grizzled, and one young and good looking. They'd question him. The grizzled one would be mean and controlling, and the more attractive one would say that he really had Jacob's best interests in mind. As for his part, Jacob would tell them the truth. He was under the influence of Bill. It was Bill who had killed both Emily and Mark Benjamin. Yes, maybe Jacob had acted hastily trying to dispose of the car, but he was only doing what anyone would do in a situation like that. Surely they'd understand.

Though, as the track-suited man walked into the room, alone, he doubted that anyone would understand. Things were already stranger than they were on TV.

"Jacob Kingsley, right?" the man said, placing a notepad down on the table. Jacob sat up in his seat, trying to see what was written on it. He thought he got a glimpse of an anime girl in the *Moe* style, but he must have been mistaken.

The tracksuited man quickly pulled the pad towards his end of the table, concealing it from Jacob's view. He held it at his side, glancing down at it briefly as he spoke. "Why'd you say that you went on that date with Miss Grainger?"

"Who?" Jacob asked.

"Emily. Miss Emily Grainger."

"Because I did."

"Uh huh," Robert said curtly.

"You're the guy who came to my house yesterday, right?" Jacob said.

"Yes. I was hoping we could avoid all of this, but you didn't want to cooperate."

"I'm cooperating. I'll tell you everything."

"Good," Robert said, genuinely pleased that the interrogation was going so smoothly. He hadn't had this easy of a time with it since the eighteen-year-old prostitute they had squeezed for information on a coke dealer. She had cried and cried, spilling name after name. It had only cost the department four boxes of tissues. Of course, that was years ago— back when he was still getting cases.

"So, tell me," Robert said, "where is Emily now?"

"What?"

"You torched her car out there. Burnt it all up, so I think it's safe to say she's not in a good way. Am I right in assuming that, Jacob?"

"Yeah."

Robert pulled the chair from the wall, put it at the table across from Jacob, and sat down. "So, tell me what happened."

"I'm not sure. I haven't seen her."

"You haven't seen her?"

"No, sir."

"Not since your date, you mean."

"What?"

"Your date Saturday night. You mean you haven't seen her since you kissed her goodbye at her doorstep."

"That's right," Jacob said, wishing that he hadn't squashed Bill. Murderer or no, Bill was great at getting him out of tight situations.

"Well, what if I told you that we searched your house. Would your story change then?"

"He's bluffing," Bill said, the familiar voice coming from just beyond his ear canal.

"Bill, you're alive!" Jacob shouted.

"What'd you say?" Robert shouted back.

"Of course I'm alive. I told you, it'd take more than that to kill me," Bill laughed. "This asshole's bluffing. He doesn't have his warrant yet. He's trying to get you to admit something you didn't do. Just stay quiet and I'll take care of you."

"I never doubted you, Bill," Jacob said, fawning like a school-girl. "I'm sorry I squashed you. I didn't mean to."

"It's perfectly alright, Jacob. I was just giving you time to cool off. I'm sorry for killing those two. I know you liked them both so much."

"What the hell are you talking about, Mr.

Kingsley?" Robert asked, rising to his feet, concern growing wildly across his face.

"I definitely liked Emily, but you can keep that Mark Benjamin. He's filth—a blasphemer—right, Bill? That's what you said."

"You're right, Jacob. That's what I said."

Jacob stood to his feet as Bill materialized, landing on his shoulder just as before. His compound eyes were brighter now, and his body seemed to gleam like onyx. He was comfort incarnate, and Jacob smiled.

"We can go back now, right, Bill?" Jacob said. He was already picturing the pixelated heads of his victims exploding on *Call of Violence*, and he could practically taste the beer on his tongue.

"Of course we can," Bill replied.

Robert pushed Jacob back with both his hands, but the man was too enormous to contain. "Little help in here," he began calmly, but soon the call grew frantic as Jacob lumbered onward, threating to pin Robert between his body and the unyielding wall. "Backup! I need backup!"

Several officers rushed into the interrogation room, and brought Jacob down to the ground.

"You won't leave me, will you Bill?" Jacob whimpered as he fell.

"Of course not," Bill replied. "I'll never leave you again."

19.

For a long while, everything was pulling and push-ing and waiting. There was so much waiting. Wait-ing was almost all there was, but sometimes a man in a pressed suit would come and stand by the bars of his cell.

"It's not looking good, Jacob," he'd say one day.

"They found your little hideaway in the closet," he'd say the next.

"I'm not getting paid enough for this," he'd throw in after almost every sentence. Jacob was never certain who was paying him, but he just knew it was Bill. Bill was always looking after him.

It was Bill who kept him company in his lonely cell all that time. Together, they'd sing songs, tell jokes, and even write a little poetry if they were feeling creative. When the guard came in with the tray of food, Bill would take his place at the side of the tray, lapping up the grease on the tan piece of meat or slurping up microscopic portions of the creamed corn. At night, he'd sleep gently tucked into the folds of Jacob's neck. Sometimes, he'd even snore—a gentle, buzzing kind of snore. Jacob found it comforting.

The man in the pressed suit returned one day, as he usually did. This time he was accompanied by two guards and Jacob's sister, Natalie. Jacob hadn't seen her since his exodus west.

"Natalie," he said, gripping the bars of the cell tight with both hands.

Natalie viewed the gesture, which only seemed to make her already red eyes redder. Tears flowed freely, then.

They pained him deeply. He had never seen his sister cry, not even when their mother died. She was always so strong.

The door to his cell slid open and the guard nearest him slapped a pair of handcuffs on his wrists. "Where are we going?" Jacob asked, but his question was not answered.

"It should be a short trial," the man in the pressed suit said to Natalie. "I'll need a check by the end of it."

Natalie nodded, tears streaming down her cheeks.

The guards led Jacob and his party past the rows of inmates. Many of them jeered, laughed, or spat as he passed, despite the commands of the guards to keep quiet. He could feel a fierce nervousness creep up inside of him, and looked to Bill, who still sat on his shoulder, to keep it down.

"It'll be fine, Jacob," he said. "It'll all be over soon."

Jacob nodded, and looked straight ahead.

He was placed in a van and driven to a large, rectangular building in the center of a city block. Inside, he passed through two sets of doors until he was brought at last into a courtroom with wooden benches on one end, and a set of intricate podiums on the other. The guard told him to take a seat by the man in the well-pressed suit, and Jacob did, eyeing the man nervously. The man gave a quick smile in response, and hurriedly rose to his feet with a look of surprise. Jacob turned and saw the whole room rising with him, and he did the same.

As he stood to his feet, he noticed that he was in line at the Lenny's Diner down the street from the factory. There was only an elderly woman in front of him, and he was waiting patiently with his check in hand to pay at the register at the front of the restaurant. The cashier was a brown-haired man in a tracksuit, and he nonchalantly handed the old woman her change before looking up at Jacob and beckoning him forward with a lazy twitch of his neck.

Jacob smiled, and handed his ticket to the man. The man glanced at it, looked up at Jacob, and laughed. "Jeez, you've got quite a tall order here, don't you?"

"Pardon?" Jacob said.

"Well, just look at this thing!" the cashier said, unrolling the check until it reached the floor and threatened to stretch all the way to the front door. "We've got battery and assault on an old woman, grand theft auto, arson, disposing of evidence, two accounts of murder, being an awful boyfriend, not listening when people ask you to pay attention, not calling your mother enough when she was alive, not helping your sister out when she needed you, self-ishness, drinking too much, downloading too much online pornography, several thousand counts of masturbation, many utilizing members of the vege-table family in perverse and unnatural ways…"

The man droned on, and Jacob could hear the mighty *deet*, this time seeming to come from the center of his chest. "No, no, that's not me!" Jacob said. "That's not mine!"

The cashier gave him a snide, condescending look. "Then whose is it? This is your bill, right?"

"No, no. It's—it's the damn fly's!" the words were true and right. It was the fly's. It was always the fly's. It had been the fly's for as long as Jacob could remember. "Bill him," Jacob cried desper-ately. "Bill Bill, I mean. Bill the fly!"

The cashier shook his head with a smirk, a very Mark Benjamin-esque smirk, and handed the check back to Jacob, who took it feebly into his hands.

If you'd like to support the author and his craft, please follow him on facebook and twitter, leave him a favorable review wherever his works are sold, and tell your friends and family about *Bill the Fly*.

You can write to him at:
nategutman.author@gmail.com

Thanks for reading.